PRAISE FOR T  **RIES**

THE CASE OF ...

"The Muskrats feel like the kind of real kids that have been missing in children's books for quite some time."

—QUILL & QUIRE

"Chickadee's rez-tech savvy pairs well with her cousin Otter's bushcraft skills, and, along with Atim's brawn and brother Samuel's leadership, the four make a fine team.... An Indigenous version of the Hardy Boys full of rez humor."

—KIRKUS REVIEWS

"[A] smart and thought-provoking mystery for middle grade readers."

—FOREWORD REVIEWS

THE CASE OF THE MISSING AUNTIE, BOOK TWO

"*Missing Auntie* is a good read, with an emotional punch, and I can hardly wait for the Mighty Muskrats to take their next case."

—JEAN MENDOZA, AMERICAN INDIANS
IN CHILDREN'S LITERATURE (AICL)

"A compelling 'urban bush' adventure that offers light and reconciliation to dark truths."

—KIRKUS REVIEWS

"[D]elivered a surprising end to the story, one that left me envious of the close family ties Chickadee and the boys enjoy."

—THE MONTREAL GAZETTE

THE CASE OF THE BURGLED BUNDLE, BOOK THREE

"Cree characters who are believable, likeable, and never stereotypical…a really engaging mystery."
—JEAN MENDOZA, AMERICAN INDIANS IN CHILDREN'S LITERATURE (AICL)

"A much-needed #OwnVoices story centered on First Nations characters and culture."
—SCHOOL LIBRARY JOURNAL

"An engaging, quickly paced mystery, exceptional in its portrayal of the kids' rez humour, community relationships and traditions of teaching and learning."
—THE TORONTO STAR

"With realistic dialogue, lots of rez humour and plenty of intrigue, Hutchinson tells a good story that also instructs us on the history of the treaties and the importance of ceremony."
—THE WINNIPEG FREE PRESS

"…the book educates as it entertains."
—LIBRARY MATTERS

"…highlights issues faced by Indigenous peoples, gives glimpses into their culture and life on a reserve. This book would be an asset to any library."
—ANISHINABEK NEWS

THE CASE OF THE RIGGED RACE, BOOK FOUR

★ Forest of Reading Silver Birch Award Finalist
★ Named one of The Canadian Children's Book Centre's
  "Best Books for Kids & Teens" 2023

"The best feature of these books is the delightfully natural quality
of the Muskrat characters. In both dialogue and action, they come
across as loyal, intelligent, funny and extremely realistic."

—THE WINNIPEG FREE PRESS

"What an adventure they have, finding themselves in many
dangerous situations with many supporters offering help....
A great mystery to help us build our curious minds. Kids can make
a difference."

—DR. LAURA HORTON FOR GOODMINDS

"We all know young people like the Muskrats.... They are the type
of enthusiastic youngsters that one would love to see storming
into a classroom: excited about learning, keen to solve mysteries,
bubbling with questions, and determined to find their way in life.
They each have special talents and ways.... The Muskrats banter
and joke but are never mean. They are independent but have deep
respect for the teachings of the Elders and strive to learn and live
by traditional values. They are loyal, educated, and full of fun,
and young people can enjoy them, learn from them, and imitate
them.... This is an excellent resource for Indigenous youth, parents,
and educators. There are also lessons for all."

—THE MIRAMICHI READER

≪← A MIGHTY MUSKRATS MYSTERY →≫
BOOK FIVE

THE CASE OF THE PILFERED PIN

MICHAEL HUTCHINSON

Second Story Press

Library and Archives Canada Cataloguing in Publication

Title: The case of the pilfered pin / Michael Hutchinson.
Names: Hutchinson, Michael, 1971- author.
Series: Hutchinson, Michael, 1971- Mighty Muskrats mystery ; 5.
Description: Series statement: A Mighty Muskrats mystery ; book five
Identifiers: Canadiana (print) 20230515517 | Canadiana (ebook)
    20230515525 | ISBN 9781772603705 (softcover) | ISBN
    9781772603781 (EPUB)
Subjects: LCGFT: Novels.
Classification: LCC PS8615.U827 C3675 2024 | DDC jC813/.6—dc23

Copyright © 2024 by Michael Hutchinson
Cover © 2024 by Gillian Newland

Edited by Kathryn Cole

Printed and bound in Canada

*Second Story Press gratefully acknowledges the support of the Ontario Arts
Council and the Canada Council for the Arts for our publishing program.
We acknowledge the financial support of the Government of Canada
through the Canada Book Fund.*

Published by
Second Story Press
20 Maud Street, Suite 401
Toronto, Ontario, Canada
M5V 2M5
www.secondstorypress.ca

This book is dedicated to my late auntie, Virginia Arthurson. She was a teacher through and through. She spent over forty years of her life improving educational opportunities for First Nation youth. I can honestly say I would not be the man I am or have had the jobs I have had if it was not for my auntie Virginia being a trailblazer and a role model.

CHAPTER 1

Factory Flare-up

"You can't trust Indians in land deals!!"

Chickadee's eyes went wide as she looked around at her cousins. "Can he say that?"

Wincing, Sam rubbed his jaw. "He just did."

The four Mighty Muskrats were wearing aprons as they refilled the coffee supplies on the table at the back of the Factory Hall. The room was half-filled with members of the Windy Lake First Nation. The other half was made up of Canadian citizens.

Sam's brother, Atim, the tallest of the Muskrats, shook his head, sending his new, braided ponytail wagging. "That makes me mad. Shouldn't he be in trouble for that?"

Otter, the smallest of the team, looked over his shoulder at the crowd erupting into applause and jeers as the man made his accusation. "I don't think that's going to happen."

Samuel ran his fingers through his short, black hair. "The cottagers are supposed to be able to table their issues with the new lease agreement. That's why Windy Lake held this meeting, but I didn't think it would turn out like this!"

The Windy Lake Factory Hall was one of the oldest buildings in the area. It was constructed of limestone brick from a nearby quarry and great wooden roof beams from the nearby forest. The First Nation had rented the grand hall for this meeting, now echoing with cottagers' calls to reject the new deal. The stage held the angry man at the podium as well as the Chief and Council sitting grimly behind him.

Pounding the dais with one hand, the silver-haired man pushed his glasses up his nose with the boney index finger of his other hand. His harangue continued. "The First Nation will tell you that they are the owners of that land! But where is the evidence? The treaty is vague. Nobody knows where the haylands mentioned back then started and stopped! Why should we accept their word that they own the land?"

Atim was incredulous. He punched the palm of his left hand. "Who *is* that guy?"

Just then, the Muskrats' favorite older cousin walked up, clipboard in hand. Due to her years as an activist for her community, Denice's passion and bravery were well-known. Recently, her leadership among teens and young adults had earned her a job with a Windy Lake Councillor.

She'd helped organize the meeting and had asked the Muskrats to clean and set up the Factory Hall. Her jean jacket had been replaced by a gray blazer. Her long, black hair was pulled back tight, the ponytail wrapped with dark green cloth.

Denice rolled her eyes before she answered Atim. "That's Hayter Scott. He represents the cottagers. He's being over the top, so I guess he's doing his job. It's politics. But now it is getting dangerous. The land does belong to Windy Lake, but there really is no way to prove it."

Sam scowled. "That doesn't sound right. Wouldn't there be papers and stuff?"

Denice nodded. "There were, but they were all kept in the Indian Agent's house, and that burned down a long time ago. The treaty in the Ottawa archives does refer to the haylands as being the edge of the reserve land. But where did they define the edge of the haylands? We really don't have anything official."

The man at the podium said something about the cottagers being the true developers of the area. "That land would still be nothing but bush if it wasn't for us!"

Half the audience put their fists in the air and cheered.

Chickadee finished replenishing the coffee sticks and sugar packets on the table. "Why are they so angry?"

Denice closed her eyes and took a deep breath. "Well, when the lease agreement was made, Windy Lake was under the control of an Indian Agent. That guy gave the cottagers fifty-year leases for five dollars apiece. Each cottager has been using our land for the past fifty years for the five dollars that went straight to the Indian Agent. It was a sweet deal. With the new lease proposal, they'll now have to pay hundreds of dollars per year to keep their cottages."

Sam lifted an eyebrow as he stacked napkins on the table. "I guess I would be mad too, but they must realize what a deal they've had all this time."

Denice shrugged. "You'd think they'd be grateful. And really, the First Nation is just going to charge them current market value for the use of the land. But what's probably going to happen is that the cottagers will take us to court."

An extra-angry growl from the crowd caused them all to turn toward the podium.

Hayter Scott had his fist in the air. "I *know* they have no proof of ownership to those lands. It's about time we brought an end to these race-based laws and make sure everyone is treated equal!"

Denice scoffed as she turned to her cousins. "There are no race-based laws. But there *are* history-based laws. We couldn't help but be a different people at first contact. That's a matter of history. And really? If we were Caucasian at first contact, like the Settlers, do you think we would *not* have the Indian Act? We still would. But it's about controlling the land and the original owners of these lands. It's not about race at all." She looked up as the crowd cheered again.

In a raised voice, Hayter addressed his side of the room. "Without proof, we owe them nothing!"

With tight lips, Denice looked at her younger cousins. "You want to hear something rich? Guess who is the old Indian Agent's son?"

Chickadee's eyebrows rose. "You don't mean…?"

Denice nodded. "Yes. The reason Hayter knows there's no evidence? His dad was the old Indian Agent. The house he lives in was his father's second house after the first one burned down. It's huge. He's been around here for as long as Grandpa."

Atim snapped his fingers. "I bet Grandpa is going to get up and tell this guy what's what."

The other Muskrats agreed.

Otter snickered. "I saw Grandpa come in, and he looked loaded for bear. All fired up."

Chickadee smiled, proudly. "Grandpa will for sure speak."

A perplexed look had been stamped on Samuel's face. "Denice, I still don't get that there's no proof about the border of the reserve lands."

Denice responded with a shrug. "There was a thing called a surveyor's pin. It was like a big spike they'd hammer into the ground to mark their land measurements. I was told the pin had the boundary of the reserve etched into its head. The haylands were really muskrat fields, mostly swamp, back then. That's why we got that land.

The oral history is that Canada's surveyor didn't want to walk in the swamp, so he just hammered the pin into the biggest rock near the reserve edge. He etched the actual borders into the top of the pin."

Atim slapped his forehead in consternation. The other Muskrats chuckled.

Their older cousin shook her head. "Not too funny, because that pin was stolen a long time ago." With her pen, Denice pointed out through the back doors of the room. "From here, in fact. You know that big display case in the lobby?"

The Muskrats nodded in unison.

"Well, it went missing from there," Denice told them.

Sam's brow furrowed. "How did it get from where it was nailed into the rock to the display case?"

Denice tilted her head and sighed. "When did everything change around here? When they built the dam for the mine. The haylands were swampy to begin with. The dam held back the river, but that raised the levels in the streams that flowed through the swamp, eventually flooding it completely after the dam was finished. They pulled the pin then because nobody knew how much the water would rise."

Otter grimaced. "Grandpa told me that the ancestors wanted those swampy fields because they were full of muskrats. In tough times, we could sell their fur and eat their meat."

"So, what happened after the flooding, you know, settled down?" Atim wanted to know.

Otter took off his hat, scratched his head, and then put the hat on again. He looked at Atim, "The muskrats left, and a new lake was formed."

"And that's when the Indian Agent built himself a big home on the new lake. Then he surrounded himself with Canadian cottagers so he'd have his own little neighborhood," Denice concluded.

Hayter Scott's supporters rose to their feet, clapping and cheering, as he finished his speech.

Chickadee could see her older cousin stiffen as the cottagers and their supporters welcomed Hayter back into their midst. Denice had spent years protesting the negative environmental and social impacts of the mine and dam.

The microphone squealed as the emcee of the meeting awkwardly thanked Hayter for his comments.

Denice looked at the stage. Her employer, a Windy Lake Councillor, was motioning for her to come see him. She smiled and indicated she was coming. "We'll talk more later. Thanks for helping out, guys." Denice slipped away through the crowd.

Atim, Sam, and Otter began to take off their aprons, but Chickadee held up a hand. "Wait! We have to stay until the meeting is over, at least. Don't you want to hear Grandpa?"

With a hesitant nod, the boys left their aprons on.

Over the next hour, people from both sides of the argument walked up to microphones placed in the aisles to express their concerns. Those on the cottagers' side mirrored their leader's message. The few First Nation people that got up wanted to ensure that the Chief and Council spent the money from the new leases in a good way, for the families and children of Windy Lake.

As time passed, the Muskrats grew more and more surprised that their grandfather hadn't approached a microphone or even been invited to the stage. As they went about their work, they would wander by where Grandpa was sitting in his beaten hide jacket and jeans, his long, silver hair in a braid. He was nestled in a garden of aunties.

Otter was the last to check out the family patriarch. "He looks angry, but he's still not getting up."

Chickadee puffed up her round Cree cheeks and then blew out the air. "Well! That doesn't make sense to me. Grandpa always speaks up for our people."

Atim tossed his braid over his shoulder with a flick of his head. "I thought he would for sure, especially after what that Hayter said."

Samuel shrugged. "We can ask him about it later, I'm sure. But the meeting is almost over. I really want to check out that display case. Let's start cleaning up now, so we have time to look at it carefully before the hall is closed."

The other Muskrats agreed and began cleaning up as much as they could before the meeting finally adjourned. They had always been inseparable. They had been given the name Mighty Muskrats by their oldest uncle, who had watched them laugh, fight, poke, and snap at each other as they grew up. The nickname had spread across the First Nation, and each of their exploits added to the Mighty Muskrats' reputation.

The atmosphere was tense as the speeches and questions ended, spurring the leadership to shuffle everyone out of the room as quickly as possible.

Once all the chairs were stacked, the sleuths waved good-bye to the janitor and stepped out into the large Factory Hall lobby. The walls were made of thick wood planks that branched off into more hallways full of bathrooms, smaller meeting rooms, a kitchen and canteen, offices, and the janitor's utility room. The display case stood opposite the building's front doors near the entrance to the hall. Its beige paint fit in with the surrounding lack of color, the wood thick and chunky, and its form was practical rather than artistic. The first section had no shelving from the case's bottom to its top. Inside was an ancient dress with plaques and pictures that told its story. The other two sections held varying-sized shelves filled with framed photographs, trophies, ribbons, and knickknacks of historical significance.

Chickadee touched the yellowed glass of the case, studying the ancient piece of clothing on display. "What a beautiful dress. The plaque says it belonged to a Métis lady who lived here way back during the fur trade."

Atim knocked against the wood. "How do you get into this thing?"

Sam studied the front frame. "Trophy cases have doors so you can get in from the front, but you can see the wall through these shelves. Maybe the case opens at the back, too." He flicked the tiny brass lock that kept the shelved objects secure.

Otter was closely observing the cabinet's construction. "I think you can only get to the dress display from the back. The whole thing looks like it's been here for a long time."

Chickadee was still reading about the story of the dress. Distracted, she mumbled, "It's dusty. Someone should take it out and clean it."

Atim attempted to lift one end of the case, but figured it was futile before he started. "No wonder that display hasn't been changed in a while. This thing is a hulk. You'd need at least two strong people to move it out from the wall."

Sam was now on his knees, his head resting against the floor as he studied the area underneath the case between its massive legs. The brown paint of the wall, the cracks between the boards, and a thick layer of dust was all that he could see. "I'm not sure we're going to find any clues here about where the pin is now."

Atim sighed heavily. Looking at the ceiling, he moaned. "But we *are* looking for it, right?"

Samuel chuckled.

Chickadee slapped Atim on the shoulder. "It's spring break next week. What else you got to do?"

Atim shook his head. "Nothing! I was *really* hoping for nothing."

Otter reached his arms around the shoulders of the two brothers. "It looks like the Mighty Muskrats are on the case!"

Sam gathered Chickadee in, and they all formed a circle. "Yes! We're on the Case of the Stolen…no, Pilfered… Pin!"

CHAPTER 2
Golden Rumors

The bell above the door of the House-taurant jingled as Atim and Sam stepped into the home business.

Mavis, the large First Nation woman who owned the place, rolled her eyes upon seeing them. "*More* Muskrats!?"

A voice from the kitchen responded, yelling, "Oh, no!" Undoubtably, it was one of Mavis's daughters, who had a smidgen less mirth and girth than her well-known mother.

Wanting to make a living in a community with few buildings and little infrastructure to support a business, Mavis had moved herself and her two daughters into the basement. Then she'd pulled out the carpet on the first floor, replaced it with linoleum, scrounged up some tables and chairs, bought the large freezer humming in the corner, and opened an eatery. She was the best advertising on the quality and quantity of her homemade fare.

Without giving the brothers a chance to respond, Mavis lip-pointed. "Your cousins are in the corner." She turned and continued to deliver coffee and gossip to the other customers.

Her warm welcome inspired big grins from the boys. They both knew Mavis teased them because she was a caring Cree.

Chickadee and Otter were already at the table, their outdoor clothing slipped over the back of their chairs. Chickadee's smile beamed from between her plump cheeks. Her long, black hair hung down, unbraided, but tied.

Otter tipped his cap, giving the haircut his grandfather had given him a moment to spring out like porcupine quills, before being flattened as the hat was put back on. The motion and the quick nod that followed reminded the brothers of their uncles.

Atim and Samuel removed their spring coats, draped them over the chairbacks, and slid into the seats.

The older brother grabbed the single-page menu that they all knew by heart. "Order yet?"

Otter shook his head, pointing to the cups in front of them. "Just a couple of herbal teas, so far."

Atim snorted. "So grown up."

Chickadee smacked his hand. "I like tea. Reminds me of Grandma."

Otter grabbed a bottle from the condiments basket and squeezed a dollop of golden goo into his cup. "I like honey. But you're not allowed to drink it right from the container."

Samuel rapped his fingers on the table. "Let's order quick so we can get to the case. I've been thinking, we should...."

Atim held up a hand. "Food first. I'm going for the cheeseburger and fries."

Mavis stepped up just as he spoke. Absently, she wrote on her notepad. "One cheeseburger and fries. Tea?"

Atim grabbed the honey container, and gave it shake to make sure Otter had left some for him. "Sure. Why not?"

Chickadee and Otter agreed to share a two-egg breakfast with scrambled eggs and a slice of ham.

When it was his turn, Sam smiled up at Mavis.

The older woman raised an eyebrow. "Oh, boy. What do you want, you little charmer?"

Sam smiled. "You ever hear about the pin that was used to mark the edge of the rez?"

Mavis was obviously taken aback by the question. She pulled out a chair at the neighboring table and sat down. "People have been talking about that big nail since I was a little girl. All the bad stuff that has happened to Windy Lake started when that pin was moved. Some people say it's cursed. But let me tell you...."

The Muskrats knew that phrase went right to the eatery owner's core, and they were about to be regaled with a gallon of gossip. They leaned in.

14

"…some people say it was solid gold." Mavis's eyes got wide at the thought. "When they were making the treaty, the Treaty Commissioner gave the gold to the Chief, who had it made into the pin. Other people say it doesn't only have the boundary of the reserve on it, but also the location of the cache to end all caches, full of a whole village of goods—teepees and all. Other people say it's just an ordinary surveyor's spike—brass or something. I like to think it was gold. But if it was gold, I bet it's gone for good. Can you imagine? What you could do with that!" Mavis let out a low whistle.

"So, who do you think took it?" Sam asked.

Mavis shook her head sadly. "Nobody really knows. It happened a long time ago, long before your parents and I were around. There's Elders who would know the stories, for sure."

Chickadee's lips tightened. "So, no suspects?"

Mavis looked at her out of the corner of her eye. "Nah! I wouldn't say that. Rumor has always been that Hayter Scott took it, way back when he was…well, way back when he was good buddies with your grandfather."

Atim gasped. "Our grandpa was friends with that guy?"

Mavis nodded. "It was when they were just young men, but I've heard it said more than once."

The Muskrats shared a shocked look with each other.

Mavis burst into chuckles. Placing a hand on the table,

she pushed herself to her feet, still chuckling. "I bet you didn't know *that* about your Elder. I got to get back to work, but if I remember anything else, I'll come back."

The young sleuths sat in stunned silence.

Then they all began to speak at once.

"Who the…?"

"How the…?"

"Why the…?"

"What the…?"

They all burst into chuckles.

Mavis dropped off two more teas and left just as quickly.

Atim and Sam dipped their teabags into the steaming water.

Chickadee tapped the edge of the table with her hand. "Seems like we have a lot of questions for Grandpa."

Atim snickered. "Or we could just skip those questions…for now. Grandpa didn't seem to want to challenge that Scott guy at the meeting last night. Who knows if he'd get mad at us for asking."

Otter blew on his hot tea. "I want to find the hole that pin was in."

Atim's forehead crinkled. "Why? The pin wasn't in the hole when it was lost."

Otter shrugged. "Now that I know it's out there, I just want to find it. You know, if it was on the last piece of exposed bedrock before the cottagers came, it would be at

Picnic Creek Point, wouldn't it? Where we go sliding on the chute?"

Sam nodded. "Yeah, that sounds right. Maybe we should head out there."

Mavis sidled up with their plates. She expertly dealt out the food. "Eat up, Muskrats. You're all too skinny. I don't know how you stay warm in the winter."

Sam smiled up at her. "By thinking of you and your great cooking, Mavis."

The restauranteur's cheeks turned red. "Charmer!" She giggled and reclaimed her seat at the empty table. "You kids are too young, but has anyone ever told you about the Indian Agent?"

Sam waggled a hand. His other held a fork full of food. "We've heard some things. That guy was like their mayor and boss and warden, all in one. The Indian Agent system made sure the First Nations didn't get to elect the main decision-makers in their own communities."

Mavis's eyes widened. "The power those Indian Agents had! They could decide not to let kids come home from residential school. They decided if a First Nation person could sell their cows or fish or hay. They even adopted out First Nation children."

Atim's mouth was full. "Day wood oose da do dent adainst da barens!"

"Man!! You're spraying cheese and cow all over the table," Chickadee scolded her cousin.

Mavis shook her head. "What?"

"He said, they would use the students against the parents," Otter interpreted. "I think he means in residential school."

Mavis nodded. "Hayter Scott Senior was known for that. I heard he even arranged marriages among people he thought were 'good Indians.'"

Chickadee was astounded. "A government employee arranging marriages! How messed up is that?"

Sam whistled. "That's like experimenting with people's whole lives."

Mavis snorted. "They had total control over us. The police did whatever the Indian Agent told them to do. And that's why I think Hayter Scott Senior took the pin. To keep his control and ensure that he was in charge of whatever happened on the new little lake."

Atim grinned. "We're going to go out to Picnic Creek Point to look for the hole in the bedrock where the pin used to be."

Mavis smiled at the Muskrats, giving each a nod as she stood up once again. "I'm glad you detectives are on it. Now, there's an Elder waving his coffee cup at me. Back to work!"

While they ate, the sleuths debated which one of their older cousins would be willing to drive them out to Picnic Creek Point.

Atim waggled their phone. Atim and Sam's father had bought a new one, so he had given the boys his old one and told them to share it. They had christened the phone the Muskrats' Horn. As the oldest, Atim got to carry it. "I'm going to text Mark. Since his broken leg has healed, he always wants to get out of the house." His thumbs began to fly.

"Hey cuzzin! Take us out to Picnic Creek Point?"

Atim had time to stuff his face with a few bites before Mark's reply caused their phone to vibrate.

"What for? It's too cold to swim."

"We're looking for a hole in the bedrock."

"That's brave. You're a little young to be moving out of your parents'!"

"Ha, ha. So funny, I forgot to laugh. It's part of a case we're working on."

"Are you Muskrats going to get me in trouble?"

"No! Not today anyway. Lol."

"Okay. I'll come pick you guys up. Where you at?"

Triumphantly, Atim lifted his phone to the sky. "We got him! He's going to come pick us up right away."

CHAPTER 3
Cold Waters

The Muskrats downed their food quickly and paid. With a quick hug for Mavis on the way out, they reached the House-taurant's driveway just as their teenaged cousin was pulling up.

Mark rolled down a window and waved a thumb at the back of the vehicle. "Two in the front, two in the back."

Otter headed for the box of the truck.

The brothers played rock, paper, scissors for the front seat. Atim groaned when his rock was covered. Sam chuckled and headed for the cab of the truck.

Atim pulled a toque from his pocket, put it on, stepped on the bumper of the truck, and pulled himself up into its box. He snuggled in beside Otter, who seemed to love riding in the wind.

The gravel crunched as Mark stepped on the gas.

As they traveled, Chickadee and Samuel filled their older cousin in on the case. It was only a twenty-minute ride to where Picnic Creek met the highway, but it was another fifteen minutes down a gravel road to get to the swimming spot.

Chickadee checked on how her cousins were doing in the back. Taking in the scene, she nudged Sam to look as well. Atim had pulled up his legs and wrapped his arms around himself, obviously uncomfortable in his cool-looking but thin spring jacket. Otter smiled as the wind whistled around him, his layers of hand-me-downs keeping him warm enough to put an arm around his chilly cousin's shoulders.

Chickadee chided Sam. "Look at your brother. You're dressed warmer than him."

Sam grinned. "He wanted to play for it. I won. But I'll ride in the back on the way home."

The truck swayed and bounced as they went over the last potholes before the swim spot. The boys in the back were tossed like dice. The truck rolled to a stop in the small field that served as a parking spot.

Atim and Otter quickly jumped over the sides of the truck.

Chickadee went and gave the largest Muskrat a hug, rubbing his arms to get his circulation going. "How you doing, big guy?"

Shivering, hands deep in his pockets, Atim stood still for the hugging. "T-t-thiss n-n-new jacket isn't w-w-warm in the w-wind."

"I guess ever fancy doesn't always mean ever warm," Chickadee observed.

Otter laughed and spread the lapels of his well-worn jean jacket that covered an ancient hoodie and a few more layers of shirts and T-shirts. "Looks good though. I hate being cold, so I always wear extra layers, just in case."

Atim stuck out his tongue. "B-B-Boy Scout."

Mark came around the truck and waved a hand at the creek. "My boys are here!" He walked over to the exposed bedrock toward his friends and the fast-moving water.

Picnic Creek Point wasn't really a point of land but was one of the places where the granite bedrock poked through the limestone of an ancient lake. The hard, gray rock formed a low, uneven tabletop spotted with trees and foliage that had rooted in collected wells of black soil. Where the limestone met the granite, the rushing creek carved out a thin channel over the eons, creating a fast-moving chute that Windy Lake kids had been sliding down for hundreds of generations. A few miles downstream, on the other side of the highway, a wooded ridge almost surrounded the little lake that was fed by the creek and the backwash from the larger river. Cottages were smattered across the lakefront, the center of so much debate in Windy Lake.

Samuel used a hand to block the glare of the sun. "Looks like a couple of them teenagers are actually in the water."

Chickadee was surprised. "Ho-leh! They must be cold! The ice is hardly off the river."

Warmed up from the ride, Atim shrugged. "Looks like they're working at something. I better go help."

The Muskrats jogged over to catch up to Mark, who was already talking to four older boys. Two of the teens were standing in the rushing water, fully clothed, trying to hold their positions by scrunching their toes in their runners. The four of them had formed a human chain and were removing large stones from the natural waterslide and piling them on the bedrock a few yards away from the creek.

Mark smiled at his little cousins. "Our uncles did this, and their uncles before them, I'm sure. Who knows how far back it goes?"

Atim dipped a toe into the creek. "What are they doing?"

One of Mark's friends pointed upstream. "When the water freezes, the ice hugs the stones along the shore. Then when winter ends, the ice breaks up and pulls the stones away from the shore. The chunks of ice carry them downstream, and when the ice gets to these little rapids, it crumbles, dumping the stones right where we want to swim."

Mark nodded. "Every year, members of our families come and remove the stones." He lip-pointed at the huge pile of rocks that was increasing in size as the teens added this year's stones. "We add about ten to twenty of them every year. Imagine how long it's been going on!"

Samuel's face skewed, and he got a faraway look in his eyes. "If all the rocks in the pile are close in size to the ones from today and about twenty were collected each year, I'd guess there's probably a century's worth of stones there. Maybe more."

Mark's friend indicated part of the pile. "I think it started over there and then slowly expanded over the bedrock."

Atim called out to one of the boys in the water. "I could take a turn!"

Chickadee reached out to him. "Are you crazy? You almost froze on the way here."

"If they can handle it, I can," Atim said.

Mark chuckled. "I'll make sure the truck is warmed up before we leave. Let him freeze his toes off if he wants to."

Chickadee shrugged, resigned.

Atim stepped into the water. His face tightened as every muscle in his body tensed. After a second, he took a deep breath and blew it out quickly. "It's c-c-cold!"

The teenager he had offered to replace stepped out of the water. "I'm out now, so keep on going, Muskrat."

Bracing himself against the current, Atim took another step, then another, feeling for rocks with his feet. When he found one, he reached in and pulled it out, then struggled to hand it off to the teen waiting closer to the granite shore. After passing it along, Atim inched his way back into deeper water.

Otter had been pacing back and forth while the other Muskrats spoke to the teens. He was bent over, carefully studying the ground, making his way to the highest point of bedrock before it slowly descended to the lake.

Sam and Chickadee meandered over to their bush-wise cousin, also looking for the hole in the bedrock.

Sam spoke absentmindedly as he focused on the ground. "See anything yet?"

"No," Otter said. "But I imagine it's probably filled with dirt."

Sam's brow furrowed. "Yes, but it would be a drill hole, and it would be higher up on the rock. So, you'd think it would be easy to spot." He looked around. "This is the highest ridge of bedrock. It would make sense to put the pin here."

Otter stood up and watched Atim and the teenagers remove the stones from the creek. "Unless…."

Chickadee squinted in the sunlight but focused on Otter. "Unless…?"

Otter shrugged. "Look how the bedrock is rising just as it enters the pile of stones. The older stones are in that depression, but over the years, maybe it spilled over a higher bump."

Samuel groaned. "So, you think we have to move the stones to find the hole?"

Otter nodded. "Yeah. It's really the only big change since the dam flooded the muskrat fields and made the lake."

Chickadee whistled. "That could be a lot of work. Should we ask Mark's friends if they'll help?"

Sam nodded with vigor. "For sure, many hands make light work. We better ask quick. They were pretty much done when we got here."

As they rejoined the teenagers at the falls, the three Muskrats smiled at them with their most charming smiles. Atim was sitting on the shore with his shoes off, wringing out his soaked socks.

Mark noticed the grins on his younger cousins as they approached. With a worried look, he tapped his buddy's arm. "We're in trouble. Don't look them in the eye."

The other teen snorted. "I ain't afraid of no Muskrats."

Mark shook his head. "Just wait. They're not mean, they're cute."

Chickadee gave them a cheery wave before she spoke. "Hey guys! Thanks for keeping Picnic Creek Point safe by moving those stones."

Sam smiled, nodding in strong agreement. After a short pause, he clapped his hands. "Now! How would you like to be a part of the Mighty Muskrats' latest case?"

Mark groaned as the faces of the other teens lit up with interest.

A few short moments later, the smallest Muskrat was at the head of a human chain picking stones from the great pile that had taken generations to build. The most bush-wise of all the Muskrats, Otter was selective about the stones he removed, assuming that following the highest ridge of the covered bedrock would reveal the drill hole.

The whole team, including Atim, was complaining of sore backs and tired arms by the time Otter lifted a river-worn, squashed football of granite that sat right against the bedrock, well along the rim they'd been following. Otter gasped when he lifted the egg-shaped stone. Beneath it was an unnaturally round hole, the size of a large coin, edges slightly chipped, and filled with mud.

The other Muskrats and the teens gathered around excitedly. They congratulated each other for the hard work that led to finding an important clue.

One of Mark's friends lifted his arms in celebration. "I can't believe I helped the Muskrats with their latest case. My mom is going to be freaked!"

Atim took out the Muskrats' Horn. "I'm going to take pictures. I bet Denice and the Chief and Council will want to know we found this!"

After, everyone who could took pictures. Then they all said good-bye, hopped in their trucks, and headed back to town.

Since Atim was wet, he sat in the front with Chickadee and Mark. Samuel and Otter rode in the back, but opened the cab's rear window, so they were still connected to those inside.

Mark chuckled as he rubbed the muscles of his driving arm with his free hand. "I bet those guys are going to think twice the next time they see a smiling Muskrat."

Otter had a huge grin and had turned his cap backwards on his head, so it was less likely to be caught in the chilly, spring air. He spoke extra loud through the window over the whooshing sound of the wind. "It's pretty cool we found it. The surveyor drilled that hole, like, a hundred years ago! I've wanted to see it ever since I heard about it."

Samuel patted his cousin on the back. "Good job, Otter. If you hadn't been able to read the rock, we might never have found it."

Everyone agreed, and Otter's cheeks burned red for a moment.

Chickadee looked over her shoulder. "The Band Office won't be open until Monday, but we should for sure take your pictures to show Denice and her boss. Hey, Atim?"

Atim held out the phone. "I wish we could take them there now!" He had removed his shoes and pulled his legs up against his body for warmth. "But...where *are* we going? I need to get warm."

Mark turned up the truck's heater. "We'll keep the warm air blowing on you. You'll be almost dry when we get to town. Where do you guys want to go? I'll drop you all off in one place. I'm not driving back and forth across the rez."

Sam reached in and poked his brother. "Mom is at Saturday bingo at the Factory Hall, and I want to take another look at that display cabinet."

Mark shook his head in strong disagreement. "I ain't stopping at bingo. I'll…I'll just slow down, and you guys can roll out."

Atim guffawed. "Don't worry, she said they already had a number caller."

Mark pursed his lips. "That's the largest collection of aunties for miles around. I'm not in the mood for a scolding."

Chickadee nudged her older cousin. "Feeling guilty about something?"

"You should be thanking me for the warning, little cousins. You've never faced a room full of angry aunties with bingo dabbers, locked and loaded. If they get you to be the caller, the ones that are your *real* aunties expect you to call their numbers. If you don't, you're dead. The ones that *aren't* your real aunties? They *expect* you to call your real aunties' bingo numbers, so they hate you too. No matter who wins a game, someone is angry with you. It's a lose-lose situation."

Sam reached through the rear window and gave their driver a reassuring squeeze on the shoulder. "We'll chance it. You don't even have to turn into the parking lot at Factory Hall."

Mark shrugged, worried but resigned. "It's your skin, Muskrats. It was an honor to know you."

CHAPTER 4

BINGO and Bust!

The truck's wheels threw up gravel as Mark sped away. It was early evening when the Muskrats made their way across the Factory Hall parking lot.

Atim led the march into the lobby. "I want to see if Mom is here. She may have some dry clothes of mine in the car."

Chickadee followed closely behind. "I'm going to check in with my mom. Maybe she won something!"

As they left, Sam smiled at Otter, shaking his head. "My mom never wins anything."

"Maybe you should volunteer to be the number caller then," Otter joked.

Chuckling, they turned to study the large cabinet in the lobby once again. It seemed ancient. In the protected environment, untouched by the seasons, the wood had dried until it was almost petrified. The dusty, yellowed dress within just hinted at the cabinet's age. The trophies were filled with well-known family names that went back for generations.

Samuel slapped his face. "Did you know the town of Windy Lake, not our rez, had a golf tourney every year?"

Otter snorted. "Nope. Where would you play golf around here?"

"I don't know," Samuel said, shaking his head, "but guess who it's named after?"

Otter shrugged, hesitantly, then ventured, "Tiger Woods, maybe?"

Sam chuckled. "Nope. Hayter Scott Senior!"

Otter's lips tightened. "He sure was a big man around here."

Sam nodded. "I've never really looked at this display case before. There's a lot of info in these captions and papers."

Over their shoulder, a shy baritone began to speak. "This place was the old Hudson's Bay Company Factory."

Startled, the boys turned. The hall's janitor leaned against a mop, a pail of dirty water at his feet. The First Nation man seemed almost as old as the cabinet. His long, black hair was salted, and his brown skin was like the leather of an expensive wallet. The Muskrats' parents called him Mr. Dave.

Sam smiled at the older man. "I didn't know that. It's a great old building. The biggest hall in town!" He paused for a moment and raised a finger. "But why is it called a factory?"

The janitor took in a deep breath. "Back in the fur trading days, a factory was any place where stuff was collected or put together or distributed—sometimes all three. This was where the goods for trade were stored. From the smaller trading posts and trading trips, furs were taken in, bundled into big bales, and shipped to England."

Otter whistled. "So, this building is *really, really* old."

Mr. Dave grinned, happy to be talking about the building he obviously loved. "I've been taking care of this hall since I was a little boy. My dad was caretaker here before me. Have you ever seen the Octopus?"

The boys looked at each other, surprised.

Sam was quick to ask, "What do you mean 'the Octopus?'"

Mr. Dave picked up his mop and pail and pointed with his lips toward a set of doors that led off into a hallway. "Come with me. I'll show you."

Otter elbowed his eager cousin. "Should we wait for Chickadee and Atim?"

Sam nodded in the janitor's direction. "I still really want to check out the cabinet, but Mr. Dave is already moving. You know, maybe if we go and listen to his stories, we can gather some useful info. We can check the cabinet out after the tour."

Otter and Sam set out after the older man.

After dropping his pail and mop off by the sink in the utility room, the caretaker pulled out a ring of keys and opened a door the boys had never been through. The air that slipped out was musty.

Mr. Dave turned and smiled at the boys. He pulled on a rope hanging from the ceiling. When it clicked, a row of lights led down a very narrow set of stairs. "If you get scared, let me know," he said.

The smell of dust and mold intensified as they descended. Someone had painted the ancient planks of the stairs an industrial gray-blue. Otter shuddered as he imagined a swarm of spiders coming from the spaces between the steps. Sam tiptoed as he imagined zombie hands reaching out to grab his ankles as he descended.

Mr. Dave seemed unconcerned about his feet and began to describe the building like he was a museum guide. "Look at the floor. See that rough concrete? First concrete poured in the area. It's hard to keep clean 'cause it's so rough, but that's how they did it back then. Up here, anyway."

The concrete floor was definitely not smooth. It seemed to have been smeared on, like the icing on a cake. Years of dirt and grime were caught in its uneven surface.

Walls of tough planks and little color stretched down a wide corridor. Doors closed off unidentified rooms on either side.

Mr. Dave continued on toward the darkened room at the end as the boys followed.

The caretaker waved at the doors on either side. "These rooms used to hold fur trade goods. Some of them stored supplies."

When they reached the end of the corridor, Mr. Dave stepped into the dark room and tugged on another rope hanging from the ceiling. The light revealed a huge behemoth of concrete, steel, and tin that took up the center of the big room.

Mr. Dave held is arms wide. "The Octopus! I bet you didn't know there was an octopus in Windy Lake."

A large, cast-iron barrel, held together by huge rivets, was the body of the Octopus. It sat in a raised nest of the same smeared concrete that made up the floor. Thick, tin arms emerged from the Octopus's head and reached out to the walls in all directions.

"This was the first furnace in the area. We're on our third one now. They built things to last in the old days, so it was too much work to take this one apart. They just removed what little bit of duct work they could and covered the vents. The newest furnace is half this size and runs on electricity."

After seeing the Octopus, Sam and Otter were genuinely impressed.

Sam smacked his forehead. "Wow! That thing is huge. Did they build the building around it?"

Mr. Dave smiled, happy that the boys were interested. "Actually, they did. We have a big door that comes directly into the basement, but there's nothing big enough to get that thing down here."

Otter ran his fingers along the cold cast iron. "It must have been hot in this room when this was burning full blast."

Mr. Dave laughed. "Never thought of that. But I wouldn't know, the second furnace was installed when I was a kid."

Sam's eyebrows shot up. "Did you know our grandpa when he was a kid?"

Mr. Dave gave a nod. "Yep. He's older than me, but we're both old men."

Otter and Sam shared a look.

Sam spoke up. "You know, we're actually hoping to find the surveyor's pin that went missing from the case upstairs."

Mr. Dave looked surprised. "Oh! My dad hated that thing. Really? You're looking for that?"

Otter and Sam nodded vigorously. "Maybe we could ask you some questions about those days."

Mr. Dave pursed his lips and shrugged a shoulder. "Sure. Why not? In fact, follow me."

As they walked back the way they'd come, Sam ventured a question. "Do you know anything about who might have stolen the pin?"

Mr. Dave shook his head. "That was a long time ago. I was your age when it went missing. I remember it was a big deal at the time, but my dad didn't saying anything about who did it. Really, it couldn't have been in the display case long. They put it in there when they started building the dam, and it was gone by the time the dam was built."

Sam pinched his chin as they walked.

Otter grinned because he knew that meant his cousin was thinking hard.

Mr. Dave stopped at a door and pressed his shoulder against it. It swung open with a little effort and a loud creak. "This is the old office. Now we use it for our paper storage, files, and stuff." The caretaker stepped into the darkness and clicked on another light.

A chunky wooden worktable and a desk shared space with a wall of filing cabinets.

Mr. Dave turned and smiled at the boys. "I'm glad you young men are interested in the history of this area. We used to change the pictures in the cabinet upstairs a lot more often. I guess that ended when people stopped printing their photographs on paper."

Mr. Dave opened a filing cabinet. It gave out a squeak of metal on metal. He pulled out a bunch of old photographs and placed them on the table.

The boys began to look through the yellowed and curling pictures from Windy Lake's past.

Sam was ecstatic. "This is the power station of the hydro dam being built! Look at this. This is what the river looked like before the dam!"

Otter shook his head. "That's below where the dam is now, look at how wide it is!"

Mr. Dave was happy the boys were enjoying their jaunt through history. "I was just a boy when they were building the dam for the hydro station. But I can remember the whole town shaking when they were dynamiting the rock."

Otter was incredulous. "The whole town?"

Mr. Dave laughed. "It shook my mother's cupboards, that's for sure!"

Samuel picked up another photograph. "This looks like it was taken when they were building the Canadian part of town."

Otter pointed to the picture. "There's the Factory Hall, right there. They built the first part of the Canadian side of town around it."

Mr. Dave had found some other pictures in the files. "Here. These are the ones I thought you might want to see. When my dad was the caretaker, whoever took care of the display cabinet—could have been my mother—took pictures whenever they changed the items inside. These older pictures show the surveyor's pin in them."

Sam took them in his hands. "Oh my goodness. To actually see it!"

The boys huddled together. The photos were in black and white, the panels of the cabinet were the main focus. The dress was ever present, but the items on the shelves were rearranged or replaced from image to image. In a few, always on the top shelf, was what looked like a big, long tack.

Otter scratched his head. "That's it?"

Mr. Dave's eyes sparkled. "Yep, that's the surveyor's pin. It's like a long nail."

"It's a tad underwhelming," Sam had to admit, somewhat disappointed.

Otter nudged his arm. "Guess we can't tell if it's gold from a black-and-white picture."

Mr. Dave snorted. "Gold! Who told you the pin was made of gold?"

Sam shook his head. "He's kidding around. We knew it wasn't made of gold, but we did hear a rumor. Do you have a picture of the top of it?"

"No," the janitor said. "Who would have thought someone would take it? It's not really valuable."

Samuel's shoulders fell. "Well, the info on the head of the pin is valuable now. *Really* valuable."

Mr. Dave waggled his head as he conceded. "Yeah. I guess you're right."

Otter held up a picture of the cabinet when the pin was still in it. "Can we borrow this?"

"Sure," Mr. Dave said. "If it helps you find the pin. Bring it back when you're finished, and we'll see if we can find something else to interest you."

Samuel chuckled. "Thanks for showing us places we've never seen! Who knew we had an octopus in Windy Lake?"

Mr. Dave waved as they left.

The boys headed back upstairs, running up the steps to ensure that nothing grabbed them from the darkness below.

CHAPTER 5

Fort Fight

Keeping an eye out in case anyone might have followed them, Atim and Samuel strolled between the piles of old appliances, computers, and other electronic garbage that formed the perimeter of the First Nation's junkyard. Long before the boys were born, all the rusting vehicles scattered around Windy Lake were brought to this one location, then squished and stacked by a heavy metal compactor, which was removed once its task was done. Over the following years, vehicles of all kinds and sizes were added, unsquished, but in various stages of rusting decay. Here in the junkyard, the green of new spring was buried under the tall, dead grass of the previous year.

"So, you going to tell me or what?" Sam whispered to his brother.

Atim chuckled. "I told you last night, Chickadee will kill me if I spill the beans. Why don't you tell me what you found out?"

Sam grinned. "My story is too long. I only want to tell it once when we're all together. I won't tell Chickadee if you spill the beans."

Atim's eyes narrowed. "I'm not going to chance it. She'll know. She always knows."

Sam laughed. "She always does."

At the bingo hall the night before, with all their aunties and parents pulling them this way and that, the Muskrats had never been able to reconnect. Back at home, Atim told his little brother that Chickadee had pulled some juicy info out of an Elder, but that was that. Sam had been bugging Atim all night, begging him to say what Chickadee had found out. Atim had remained tight-lipped.

In the bright morning sun, the boys cast a searching gaze around the columns of the junkyard, then hurried to a battered, blue snow machine that looked like a van on skidoo tracks. Sitting just on the edge of the columns of stacked cars, the wooden cabin of the Bombardier was shaped like a beetle, with a small bump of a head followed by a bulbous hind end. Underneath, large steel skis took the place of front tires, and the bug-like cabin sat on a foundation of steel and rubber tracks. All of this had sunk a few inches into the earth.

The boys quickly made their way to the passenger side door. With one last glance to ensure no one was watching, they slipped into the interior of the snow van. On the inside, posters, pillows, and playthings suggested this was the fort to end all forts. However, this was just its foyer.

Sam carefully felt along the frame of a metal screen that separated the Bombardier's cabin from its rear engine compartment. Finding the hidden latch, he flipped it and swung open the grate. They were met with a rippled, round tin culvert leading out of the back of the snow van and farther into the stacked vehicles of the junkyard.

Sam gestured for his brother to climb inside.

The other end of the tin tunnel was stuck in the emergency door of a school bus that was buried among the stacks of cars. When the boys climbed out, they were greeted by their fellow sleuths, who were sitting at the other end of the long vehicle.

On one side, a couch replaced some of the bus seats, a dining table and chairs took up the wall nearest the culvert, and an ancient computer blinked on a desk that was pushed up against the facing side of the bus. Long ago, the sleuths had snaked an electrical cord to their sanctuary from a nearby hydro pole. Filling the view from the missing windshield, knickknacks and interesting items from the refuse outside covered the hood. A flipped-over trunk from a car covered the windshield and hood, sheltering the front of the bus from the outside.

Chickadee waved from a chair in front of the computer desk. "Hey! Did you tell Sam what we found out last night?"

Atim crossed the bus and sat on an incline bench that was screwed together from unmatched pieces of metal salvaged from the junkyard. He picked up a barbell from a discarded set of weights. "No!! You told me you'd kill me if I did."

Chickadee's eyes narrowed. "I know, but I have to find out if you didn't listen first, don't I?"

Atim shuddered. "You're freaking me out."

Strumming a guitar in one of the old bus seats, Otter snickered. "You're auntie-ing, Chickadee."

Chickadee gasped. "Eek! Sorry!"

Sam grabbed a chair, shaking his head. "Atim didn't tell me nothing!" He pounded his chest, "So, *tell* me!!"

The other Muskrats laughed.

Chickadee took a deep breath, readying to tell a long story. "Sooooo…when I went into bingo, my mom hardly had any numbers, so she made me sit beside her. She says I'm her lucky kid. I couldn't leave!"

Atim punched his younger brother. "That's why Mom always messes up our hair before bingo. She's rubbing our heads for good luck."

Sam scratched his shoulder. "I don't feel lucky."

Otter stared into infinity with a sad smile. "Grandma would always take these porcelain figurines…little animals." He held up his hand, the tips of his thumb and index finger about an inch and a half apart. "She'd line them up in a row above her cards. She said she got them as free gifts in boxes of tea."

Chickadee reached over and squeezed his arm. "I remember those. And…I miss Kookum, too."

"Grandpa still has those figurines in their bedroom," Sam said.

"Other than the sheets on the bed, I'm not sure a thing in that room has changed since Grandma died," Atim added.

They were all silent for a moment.

Chickadee took another deep breath. "Which is why the news I got is so…unexpected."

Sam exploded. "WHAT IS IT!?"

Chickadee lifted an eyebrow. "Well, really. Before you arrived, Otter was about to tell me what you guys found out…."

Otter giggled and began to talk, slightly slower than usual. "Welllll…we went downstairs…Mr. Dave…he wanted to show us something."

Samuel hit his cheek so hard it smacked. Then, everything they gleaned from the caretaker spilled out of him in a torrent. "Okay! Mr. Dave took us to the basement. It's smelly and dusty. He showed us the Octopus. Sounds cool. *But!* It's just a furnace. Tell you about it later. Mr. Dave worked at the Factory Hall for years, since he was a kid. His dad did, too. Why is it called a factory? Back in the fur trading days, a factory was a place where things were gathered together and stored. Mr. Dave knows a ton. He said that when he was a kid, the explosions from the dam would shake his mom's cupboards. He gave us this old picture, black and white. It's older than the mine and the dam. It has the surveyor's pin in it. Do you have it, Otter? Show them."

Otter held up the picture and then handed it to Chickadee.

Sam, out of breath, collapsed onto the couch. After a moment, he collected himself, stretched his arm out, and leaned back into the cushions. "Soooo, what did you guys find out? Anything?"

The other Muskrats were gathered around the photograph.

Chickadee lifted an eyebrow in Sam's direction. "Hey, Mr. Impatient! We're checking out the picture."

Atim moved the photo within an inch of his face. "How old is that dress? It's been in that display for how long?"

Chickadee grabbed a side of the photo and pulled it down so they could all look at it. "When I looked at the info with it, it said that it was worn by Sarah Beauvais. Apparently, she was a beautiful, very charming young lady. When the first governor held the first Spring Feast in the area, the governor's wife was back in England, so he asked Sarah to be the hostess. And when she agreed, he bought her this dress to wear."

Sam sighed. "Which has nothing to do with the case, I'm sure."

Chickadee shrugged. "You say you're interested in history, but you're only interested in the history that's important to you."

Samuel's eyes popped wide. Then he chuckled. "I suppose, you got me. But…I've been waiting all night."

Looking at Atim, Chickadee gave a slight nod in Sam's direction. "All right, tell him. It *might* stop his whining!"

Atim heaved a great big sigh. "Okay. So, Chickadee was sitting with her mom, and our mom wouldn't let me go anywhere because I was still damp from pulling rocks out of the creek. Chickadee was talking about the case. And she said that someone—she didn't name Mavis, of course—told us Grandpa and that Hayter guy were friends once."

Otter shook his head. "That still sounds so weird to me."

"Well, it sounded weird to the aunties too, and my mom," Chickadee continued. "So, they were all talking about it and how Grandpa was young once. Anyway, this lady Elder was there, and she was laughing to herself…."

Atim nudged his brother. "That's when our mom asked her what she was laughing about."

Chickadee let out a giggle. "And the Elder said she remembered that Grandpa liked a Canadian girl once!"

The boys' faces filled with surprise. "Ooohh! Grandpa had a girlfriend!"

After his tittering ended, Samuel's brow furrowed. "Why would she remember that?"

Chickadee shrugged. "The Elder said she had been one of our great-aunties' friends, and she knew them in residential school. She was with them when they came back. Except for the kids that had been scooped, like Great-Aunt Charlotte, of course. The Elder said all the girls that weren't family were interested in Grandpa back then."

Atim snorted. "Isn't Mark always saying how he can't find a girlfriend because we're related to so many girls in town?"

Otter waggled his head, weighing the idea. "It is a small town. And we are cousins with a load of people. I imagine it was worse when this place was even smaller."

"What did the Elder say after that?" Sam asked.

Chickadee snickered. "That's when she said, 'But he liked that French Canadian girl.' I think the aunties got a little mad at her for saying that. I don't think they'd ever heard of Grandpa liking anyone but Grandma. Anyway, it was pretty quiet for the rest of bingo."

Atim laughed. "Ever deadly quiet, for sure."

Sam held out his hands. "Okay. What does that have to do with the case?"

Chickadee shrugged. "Nothing, probably. But it's crazy what you'll find out when you start poking around. We're getting gossip from when Grandpa was a young guy!"

Otter rapped on the guitar, making a loud thump. "I wonder if the aunties will ask Grandpa about it?"

Atim lifted an eyebrow. "Hopefully, they're braver than we are. I'm not asking Grandpa about that stuff."

Rubbing an eye in frustration, Sam moaned. "Why would you have to? It has nothing to do with the case!"

Chickadee ran her fingers through her long hair. "Meh. You never know."

"What can we do today to forward the case? It's Sunday." Otter was anxious to get down to business.

Sam rubbed his jaw. "I'd really like to speak with Hayter Scott, but…how do we do that safely? And where can we bump into him as if by chance?"

Chickadee shook her head slowly. "That's a tough one. I hardly ever see him in town. He pretty much stays in his big house out by the cottages."

Atim snapped his fingers. "Cousin Eric said he was trying out for the firefighting crew this weekend."

"Cousin Eric? I can't believe he's trying out," Chickadee said. "Those guys work hard. If they're not out on a fire, they're cleaning up and drying equipment from their last mission. Eric is too skinny for all that."

Sam grinned. "They don't call him Minnow for nothing."

Otter put down his guitar and jumped up. "Hayter Scott is the head of the government's Emergency Services in Windy Lake! So, he may be there to supervise the tryouts!"

With a destination in mind, it didn't take long for the young detectives to pack up their things and crawl through the tunnel to the Bombardier. With a quick look through its round windows to make sure no one was about, the

Muskrats clambered out. They eagerly headed toward the Emergency Services Office. This meant leaving the reserve and going to the Canadian side of Windy Lake.

It didn't take long for the Muskrats to arrive at their destination. As they approached, a scream pierced the calm of the afternoon.

Otter's face was swept with worry. "That sounds like our cousin, Eric!"

The Muskrats broke into a run.

CHAPTER 6

Fire Crew Follies

The Muskrats' pumping legs carried them toward the source of the scream.

The three-story, red brick building of the government's Natural Resources Office dominated this section of the lakeshore. Beside it stood the much longer green, metal structure that housed the Emergency Services. The driveway was a great bay that returned to the main road, a fair-sized field of cut grass was in the middle, and a truck-filled parking lot was along the far end.

Outside the warehouse, several people were gathered in a circle, their focus on the ground in their midst. The young sleuths' arrival caught the attention of those along the edge of the group, and they turned to look.

Someone yelled, "Muskrats!!"

Samuel, completely out of breath, gave a half-hearted wave. "Hey…!"

Atim slapped his brother on the back and spoke up while Sam stopped to catch his breath. "Is anyone hurt?"

Suddenly, another scream erupted. It was followed by a loud voice bellowing, "Stop it!"

Chickadee pushed her way through the circle with her cousins close behind. "Is someone hurt?" she repeated.

Lying on the ground, Eric was in a neck brace. An emergency firefighter was kneeling beside him, attempting to bandage their cousin's knee.

Eric was laughing uncontrollably. He smiled at his cousins as he held his side. "I have ticklish knees!"

Trevor, the firefighter in charge, was in orange coveralls, and his blond hair had been recently cropped short. He threw up his hands in frustration. "I can't show the guys how to bandage a wound if you won't stay still!!"

Chickadee hid a smile behind her hand.

"Sheesh!" Atim exclaimed. "We thought you'd been hurt."

Samuel shook his head. "Someone should have found volunteers who aren't ticklish."

Trevor stood up. "Sounds like someone just 'should have'd' themselves."

Sam's smile disappeared.

Trevor continued, "Around here, if a person says 'someone should have,' they just volunteered for the job. You lie down here. You're in shock." He took a pen from his pocket and handed it to Sam, the crash victim.

"Pretend this is sticking out of you. You have a puncture wound."

Sam hesitated.

"Lie down! You're punctured!" Trevor barked.

Sam obeyed and hit the ground.

Trevor smiled down at him. "Good."

He pointed at Chickadee. "And you lie down. You just suffered third-degree burns from a helicopter crash. Not only do you have third-degree burns, but you also have a broken leg and can't sit up."

Chickadee bent one leg at an odd angle. Closing her eyes, she stuck out her tongue.

Trevor noticed. "Working it. Good job." He looked at Eric, then nodded toward Chickadee. "Eric, put the neck brace on your cousin. You're a medic now."

Otter held up a hand. "I can be injured, if you like."

Atim waved his arms. "Yeah! Me too!"

Trevor pointed at Otter. "You're bleeding from a piece of shrapnel in your belly. Lots of blood. Lie down over there and try to hold your guts in."

"What's wrong with me?" Atim waved an arm frantically.

Trevor deadpanned. "I'm sure your parents have a long list, but today you have a head wound. Go wander around in the field and pretend you're not sure what's going on."

Sam scoffed. "That won't be much of a stretch."

Trevor pointed a finger at him. "You're in too much pain to make jokes."

With injuries assigned, Trevor split the candidates into smaller groups and ordered them to respond to the fake injuries. "I want to see your first-aid skills. We need to know if you could take care of an injured teammate out in the bush."

The wannabe firefighters jumped to the task with gusto. Streamers of gauze and bandages suddenly fluttered through the air. A pair of applicants tackled Atim as, looking dazed, he wandered through the field. After a moment, he stood up again and continued to wander.

Trevor went to each group, slowing them down and giving directions, but they went off the rails soon after he left. Ten minutes later, he blew his whistle.

"Okay! Let's see what you did."

The young people backed away from their patients.

Otter's stomach wound had a generous but loose wrapping of gauze that almost entirely covered his body. He peered out through a slit in the thin fabric.

It looked as though a huge roll of toilet paper was tied to Sam's left side. A mile of bandages was wrapped in a great coil, tied to the patient with a web of gauze. The end of Trevor's pen stuck out of the roll's center.

Atim's legs had been tied together, preventing him from wandering around. He had taken that aspect of Trevor's assignment to heart, and it had taken four applicants to hold him down long enough for the other members of the team to wrap a beach-ball-sized bandage around his fake skull injury. He looked like an alien with a massive brain.

With hands on his hips, Trevor looked the boys over. He shook his head. "Well, at least you didn't giggle."

Smiling where she lay, Chickadee wore the neck brace and a well-built splint on her leg. Her tightly wound bandages effectively covered the once-exposed bits of skin.

Trevor raised an eyebrow and looked at the potential firefighters. "How come you did so good?"

"She told us what to do," one of them said.

A pained looked crossed their trainer's face. "I need a break. Let these kids loose and get them off the lot. The bosses will lose their minds if they see them." As he walked toward the Emergency Services Office, he yelled over his shoulder, "Fifteen minutes! Fifteen-minute break!"

The Muskrats were soon freed. With good-byes and high fives from the firefighting applicants, the Muskrats turned to leave.

Eric walked them out of the Emergency Services area. "I'm sure I won't be on the first team and probably not the second. But it sounds like it will be a dry summer, so all these guys will get to fight fire by the end of the season. I'm not worried. If cousin Jeff decides to fight fire, they'll snatch him up quick and let him put together his own team. He usually picks cousins."

When they got a little farther from the crowd, Sam tugged on Eric's sleeve. "We really came to see if we could bump into Hayter Scott. We want to get to know more about him."

"You thought the big boss would be here on a Sunday?" Eric laughed.

"There is always someone here. We thought we'd give it a try," Otter said.

Eric pursed his lips and blew out a lungful of air. "Mr. Scott is super prejudiced, but he's a good racist, I suppose."

Chickadee snorted. "What does that mean?"

"He treats Indians like they're naughty kids. Always talks down to us, like we're children that he's patting on the head. Doesn't matter how old the Indian is. I've seen him do it to guys my dad's age."

"You mean he's good compared to the people who are always...just...*mad* at us?" Atim said.

"Yeah, he's not one of those. He isn't angry that we exist. He just doesn't think we can do much without proper direction, and only his people know the right way to do things."

Otter lifted his hat, scratched his head, and put it back on again. "What would you do if you wanted to meet up with him?"

Eric laughed again. "Have to think about that. Never wanted to run into Mr. Scott before."

Sam gave his elbow a tap. "Come on. You must know something else about him."

Their older cousin's face scrunched as he thought. "You know he has a jewelry store in his garage, right?"

Atim pulled back. "What? That's crazy!"

Eric nodded. "Yeah, all those high-and-mighty people have some kind of side gig. His is this little store he keeps in his garage. He used to rent VHS tapes from there, but when they went out of style, he changed over to selling gold and silver jewelry."

Otter was astounded. "I never, ever heard of that."

Atim gave him a push. "Who do you know that buys gold jewelry? Everyone I know wears a necklace made of moose hide."

Chickadee piped up. "Most of the aunties have gold necklaces, my mom does. Some even have gold earrings."

Eric waggled his head. "I doubt he'd invite any brownies to his house. He's never liked us around the cottages. I'd bet it's worse now, with all the lease hoopla and the disagreement with the Chief and Council."

A yell from Trevor had them all look at the potential forest firefighters. Eric turned to walk back, but over his shoulder he shouted, "I have heard of people from the rez going up there to buy jewelry, though. What's he going to do? Say no to money?"

After a laugh, the Muskrats waved good-bye to their cousin.

Atim cupped a hand near his mouth. "Good luck with the tryouts. I'll be there in a year or…." His voice trailed off. He looked at Otter. "How old do you have to be to fight fire?"

Otter smiled. "You have to be at least sixteen."

Atim smacked his head. "Four years! I can't wait that long! Maybe I can get my mom to lie about my age when I'm fifteen?!"

Samuel laughed and slapped his brother's arm. "Mom isn't going to let one of her babies fly out to a forest fire until she is forced to."

Atim's shoulders fell as he reluctantly nodded in agreement.

The Muskrats walked along the main road. The spring air was crisp, but the wind was light. Joking and laughing, the sleuths began to hear an engine's roar as it sped toward them.

Soon after, a Windy Lake band police truck zoomed around the bend.

It pulled over to the shoulder and came to a stop beside them. "Get in, Muskrats. You're coming with me."

CHAPTER 7

Police and Protestors

The police truck bounced and rocked as it sped over a rash of potholes.

Sitting in the front seat, Otter looked back at his cousins as they rose into the air after a large bump. Wide-eyed, he asked, "Where are we going, Uncle?"

The Muskrats' Uncle Levi was a well-muscled man with short, salt-and-pepper hair. His dark blue constable uniform was crisp and recently laundered, and he wore a cap with the words *Windy Lake Police* fanned across the top. Keeping his eyes on the road, he said, "We've got a call that Hayter and the cottagers have set up a blockade on the highway. People are saying they've closed off access to Picnic Creek Point."

The Muskrats shared a smile, happy to have found a way to meet the head of the cottagers, even if it wasn't in the way they expected.

Sitting in the passenger's seat, a confused Sam asked, "Why do you need us?"

Uncle Levi chuckled. They all knew that the young detectives' efforts had caused almost as much concern and troubles for their Elders as the mysteries they solved. "Well, Hayter used to be my old boss back when I was younger and worked at Emergency Services. Nobody can get under my skin as much as that smarmy jerk…I mean, *guy*, can. I figure having a peanut gallery watching will help me keep my grouchy bear in check."

From the backseat, Atim tapped his uncle on the shoulder. "Know thyself, hey Uncle?"

The Muskrats' Elder nodded. "There's no point in escalating this situation—certainly not because of my personal feelings about Hayter Scott."

Uncle Levi pulled up where Picnic Creek Point road met the highway. With the protestors' cars parked on the shoulder of the thoroughfare, it was natural for drivers to slow down. Cars were then stopped by the cottagers, who handed them pamphlets through open windows.

Uncle Levi rolled down his window and took one. The woman who handed it to him gave him a cold smile, knowing he worked for the First Nation.

Sitting in the passenger seat, Samuel was also given a pamphlet. The folded paper proclaimed that a great injustice was happening under the noses of regular Canadians.

Uncle Levi harrumphed. "They're really going hard

on public relations. Says here 'What about the old people who have over fifty years of memories at their cottages?'"

Sam snorted as he read. "It even suggests their kids will never learn how to swim if they don't get to keep their summer homes."

Atim leaned in over his brother's shoulder. "Really? I bet half these people have pools back wherever they came from."

Uncle Levi took off his hat, scratched his head, and then put it back on. "Nobody is taking away their cottages. We just want them to pay a fair price for their use."

Sam scoffed and then read out loud, his voice rising slightly. "Says here 'We can't let this race-based injustice go unchecked!'"

Atim was incredulous. "What are they talking about? They've used that land for only five dollars since before Grandpa was a kid!"

Otter whispered, "That's our land."

Uncle Levi nodded. "Okay. When we get out of the truck, stay close to me and be quiet." The big man sighed before he opened the door. "Let's go find Hayter."

The Muskrats and their uncle piled out of the truck. The protestors around them looked slightly annoyed at their arrival.

Uncle Levi walked up to one of the cottagers who was handing out information. "Where's Hayter?"

The woman's eyes narrowed, but she nodded toward a small tent that appeared to have been set up as a temporary office.

Uncle Levi gave her a thank-you and headed toward the tent.

He stopped before entering and hitched up his belt. He looked down at the Muskrats and gave them a weak smile, then stepped into the tent. The Muskrats stepped in behind him.

"Hello Hayter," Uncle Levi's voice rumbled.

The old Canadian man looked up from his work. "Well, if it isn't Little Levi. Here to evict us? You'll need proof this is Indian land."

Uncle Levi took a deep breath and then let it out slowly.

Chickadee took hold of his large hand and smiled up at him. Her uncle's work-worn, rough skin felt rugged in her soft palm. After a moment, he grinned back at her.

Uncle Levi looked up and smiled at the very mature son of the former Indian agent. "Hi, Hayter. I hope you're keeping everyone safe."

The protest leader displayed a thin-lipped smile, but his eyes shot angry arrows. "Of course! We've been doing what's called a rolling blockade. We just want to inform people, so we hand out our pamphlets to everyone who slows down."

The band constable nodded. "Well, it is a highway, cars are moving fast. I just want people to be safe."

Hayter Scott stared at the other man for a moment. "Like I said, Little Levi, we'll take care of our own."

Atim couldn't hold back any longer. "Why do you call him Little Levi? He's huge!"

Samuel also piped up, speaking to his older brother. "I figured it was like Little John in *Robin Hood*. He was a big guy, too!"

Hayter pointed at Sam. "You're a smart one. Not just that…your uncle is a crusader. Ain't you Little Levi?"

Uncle Levi didn't answer, so Mr. Scott continued.

"He's going to save all you Natives. Going to rob from the rich and give to the poor. That's why he's in that uniform. Ain't that right, Little Levi?"

Chickadee was so angry she didn't notice how hard she was squeezing her uncle's hand. He wiggled his fingers, but then smiled down at her knowingly.

With his other hand, Uncle Levi lifted up his cap and scratched his head. "We both believe in serving our community. Don't we?"

The older man nodded grudgingly.

Uncle Levi nodded back. "So, what's with blocking the road to Picnic Creek Point?"

"We're not blocking it. People can get through us if they want to. But really, you can't prove it's your land. And if it's not your land, it's Canada."

"Okay. Well, how long do you plan to be out here?"

The old man kicked at some gravel, weighing possible answers. "We're not prepared to stay overnight. We'll be packing up before it gets dark."

Uncle Levi grinned. "Good, good. You certainly have the right to protest. Just want to ensure everyone is safe." The Muskrats' uncle turned and walked out of the tent and away from the head of the cottagers. The young sleuths followed closely behind.

Sam was the last to leave, and his feet seemed heavy as he walked. Finally, he turned. "Mr. Scott? I was wondering. Do you know anything about the missing surveyor's pin?"

The silver-haired man turned. He looked down at Samuel and his eyes squinted as he studied him. "You're one of the ones they call the Muskrats, aren't you?"

Sam nodded. His uncle and the others stopped to listen.

Hayter Scott rubbed his jaw. "Well, I wouldn't hang my hopes on that pin."

The eyebrow of the young investigator rose. "So, you know where it is then?"

Hayter Scott scoffed. "Ask your Grandpa. He knows as much as I do." With that, Mr. Scott turned his back on Sam.

Sam closed the tent flap, then saw that his uncle and the other Muskrats had heard the whole conversation. He smiled at his family. "Had to try."

CHAPTER 8
Source Shut Down

As the spring chill was burned away by the Monday morning sun, the Muskrats met at the midpoint between all their homes, where the main bush trail met the main gravel road. With the wind whooshing through the pine trees, they discussed their next steps.

"We need to talk to him." Sam kicked a stone. "Three people have mentioned Grandpa might know something. But who is going to ask him about it?"

Atim walked over to a stone and sent it rolling. "I don't want to do it. Grandpa didn't even want to get up and speak when that Hayter guy was freaking out at the meeting. Something is up with that."

The stone rolled to a stop in front of Chickadee, but she was watching a crow fly by. "Maybe we could ask him about the French Canadian girl at the same time."

Sam smacked his forehead. "So, we're going to poke at *two* touchy subjects at the same time? That doesn't sound like a good idea."

Otter walked up to the stone and kicked it down the bush trail. "Let's just go talk to him. Grandpa is Grandpa. If he doesn't want to answer, he'll say no."

Atim shuddered. "And then he'll get scary quiet."

Chickadee went to the stone on the trail. She gave it a kick and it rolled farther along. "Otter's right. Grandpa may get grouchy with us for a while, but he always forgives us."

Sam scoffed. "Eventually."

Atim nodded. "It's the time between now and eventually that gets me."

Otter walked up to the stone and sent it rolling.

It didn't take long for the Muskrats to get to Grandpa's house once it was set as their destination.

His door opened with the loud but familiar squeak. They found their grandfather sitting at the kitchen table with a cup of tea. His silver hair hung loose, falling over a plaid shirt. He peered at them over the edge of a well-worn newspaper, its headline at least a week old. "Hey, my Muskrats. Why are you all here?"

Atim, Chickadee, and Otter looked expectantly at Sam. Sam sighed.

Intrigued, their Elder folded up the paper and placed it on the table.

Samuel looked up at his grandfather with one eye squinted, like he was looking into the sun. "Well, Grandpa...you know we're looking for the stolen surveyor's pin...."

The old man nodded.

"Well, Hayter Scott said...."

Suddenly, Grandpa picked up the newspaper and smacked it against the table. "Don't!"

The Muskrats jumped. They'd never heard their grandpa bark like that before.

The old man sucked in a breath, then spoke sternly. "Don't say that name in this house." He picked up the paper and snapped it open, putting up a wall between him and the young sleuths.

Sam looked at his brother and cousins, eyes wide. They'd expected Grandpa to be grouchy, but not this angry. He ventured, "Grandpa, I didn't mean to make you mad. He just told us you might know something about the pin."

The paper shook before Grandpa said, "Don't trust anything that man says."

Sam stepped back. With his eyes, he urged Chickadee to help.

Before Chickadee could think of what to say, Grandpa spoke from behind the trembling newspaper.

"You kids have no idea what that man's family did to our people. I'm trying to have my tea and read my paper. Go outside and find something to do."

The Muskrats had been dismissed. As they left, the door closed with a disappointed squeak.

Speechless, the Muskrats headed for their next destination.

CHAPTER 9

Maps, Mounties, and Cold Cases

"There it is! The Band Office." With a sweep of his arm, Atim made a grand gesture that took in the whole building.

After the meeting with Grandpa, the young sleuths were looking for a win. No one wanted to talk about how Grandpa had reacted, so they headed to the Windy Lake Band Office to tell their cousin Denice they had found the location of the empty pinhole.

The governance hub of the Windy Lake First Nation was one of the newer structures in the area. Made of wood and stone, its architecture mimicked a circular powwow arbor with a round inner courtyard as the focal point of the building. The road-facing portion was a wall of wide windows that reflected the lake and sky in the rising sunlight. The parking lot was crushed, white limestone like most driving spaces in Windy Lake.

Bursting through the front doors, the Muskrats straightened their backs. The lobby ceiling was high and supported by great logs connected and held in place by huge nuts and bolts. The sleuths' footfalls echoed loudly in the large, open space between the columns of stripped tree trunks.

Behind the desk, a First Nation receptionist swiveled in her chair. A set of earphones with a thin microphone pointing toward her mouth was partially hidden under her thick hair. As the Muskrats walked up, she was greeting callers. "Windy Lake First Nation. Can you hold please? Windy Lake First Nation. Can you hold please?"

The boys stood back and let Chickadee speak to the receptionist. Chickadee smiled her biggest smile at the woman, then waited as another caller was put on hold.

"Can I help you?"

"Yes. Is it possible to see Denice?" Chickadee smiled wider.

The receptionist pointed over her shoulder as she reached for another call. "They just finished a meeting in the Council Chambers. Go on in."

Looking around, Chickadee saw huge, slightly arced hallways leading away from each side of the lobby. Numerous doors hinted at offices along their length. Spotting a set of double doors, sandwiched between rough-wood carvings of an eagle and a jumping fish, Chickadee flicked a finger, letting her cousins know they should follow.

The boys took a few quick steps to catch up. Sam leaned toward her, whispering, "Where are we going?"

Chickadee smiled. "The Council Chambers, of course."

Atim slapped Otter on the back. "The Council Chambers!"

The cousins had been to the Band Office numerous times, but it was usually with their Elders or parents as they visited the many services available at the only office building in town. Besides the First Nation's Political Office and Council Chambers, the local Education Authority, the Child Welfare Agency, the tiny Windy Lake Pharmacy, the Post Office, the Unemployment Support Office, and the First Nation's only ATM machine were all squished within the building's interior.

To be invited into the Council Chambers of the Windy Lake First Nation was an unexpected treat. All the Muskrats were excited. As they approached, the Councillor their cousin worked for left the room with a group of office workers in tow. Denice wasn't with them.

After waiting for them to pass, the Muskrats stepped into the decision-making center of the Windy Lake First Nation.

Atim looked around. "I've always wanted to see inside here."

The rest of the Muskrats nodded, eager but speechless.

The room was large. But its centerpiece, the huge, carved wooden table where the Windy Lake Council made their decisions, didn't look too big for the grand space. Portraits, paintings, and photos covered three of the walls, while flip charts, projector screens, and audio speakers dotted the fourth.

"Muskrats!" a woman's voice cut through the air.

The sleuths turned in the direction of the greeting. Their cousin Denice was on the far side of the council table. She had a laptop and file folders under one arm and held a full coffee mug in the other. Her long, black hair hung loose over a mauve pantsuit.

The Muskrats hurried up to her.

Chickadee and Denice leaned into each other, and Sam beamed broadly.

"Hey, cousin! We got good news!"

Otter gave Denice a one-arm hug, before calling Atim back. He had stepped away to look at the First Nations artwork and sculptures that lined the walls of the room.

In a rush, Chickadee and Sam told Denice about finding the hole that the surveyor's pin would have sat in before it was removed. Sam grabbed the Muskrats' Horn from his brother and showed the pictures to his older cousin.

Denice put down her files and coffee, then opened her laptop. "Do you think you could point to where it was if you saw an overhead photo?"

Otter nodded. "Pretty sure. You got one?"

Denice grabbed a cable that was lying across the table and plugged it into the computer. A moment later, Denice's desktop appeared on the large projector screen that took up a big section of one wall. She clicked a few times and suddenly a bird's-eye view of Windy Lake and its traditional lands filled the screen. The map had been marked with red and green lines. Solid green lines seemed to encircle the whole reserve, and they almost encompassed the cottage area, but there they became dotted. The red lines marked off chunks of land farther out from the Windy Lake community.

Atim slapped his forehead. "Is that ever cool!"

"Almost makes you feel like you're flying," Otter said.

"It's from a satellite," Denice told him. "You'd have to hold your breath pretty good if you wanted to fly that high."

Sam squinted at the screen. "Why did the Chief and Council need this?"

A woman's deep voice came from the back of the room. "We use it when we discuss our land use study, and of course, our land claims."

A tall native woman had stepped in from the lobby. She wore a salmon-colored blazer, a fluffy, white blouse, and blue jeans. Her salt-and-pepper hair hung just past her shoulders, and her smile brightened the room.

"The Chief!" the Muskrats gasped in unison.

Denice snickered. "Hi, Chief. My little cousins were going to show me where they found the hole where the surveyor's pin was before it was removed."

"Really?" The Chief of the Windy Lake First Nation raised an eyebrow. "We really need the info on the top of that pin. But having its original location as a point of measure could be very important, too."

Sam pointed back at the large screen. "Is that why the green arrows are dotted around the cottage area?"

The Chief nodded. "None of this would be a problem if the cottagers weren't trying to argue it wasn't our land. The treaty mentioned the edge of the haylands, but today, we don't know exactly where that falls."

Atim puffed out his chest. "Don't worry! We're on the Case of the Pilfered Pin. We'll find it."

Denice rolled her eyes, but the Chief smiled. "I feel better now that you are all on its trail."

Chickadee giggled. "Thank you for saying that, Chief."

"It's easy to give credit where credit is due," the Chief replied. "Now, show me where this hole is." She moved around the edge of the table and walked closer to the screen.

Otter quickly stepped up to the large projection of the satellite picture. He leaned in and used his finger to trace the dark line of Picnic Creek until it came to the swimming spot. The bedrock that framed the creek was a misshapen white and light gray fan set against the surrounding grass, the mottled forest, and farther away, the wide river and lake.

Otter looked over his shoulder at Denice. "Can you make this area larger?"

With a few clicks, the view seemed to fly closer to the area of Picnic Creek Point. With one final click, it zeroed in closer to the ground, causing the entire area to expand on the screen.

Atim pretended to get woozy, and he held his head. "I think I'm going to need a barf bag!"

Everyone chuckled.

Otter leaned in. "It looks different from this view, that's for sure. I think this blob here is the pile of stones that have been removed from the river over the years. What do you think, Sam?"

Samuel also leaned in. "I think so, too. And I think the bit we added is this little tail on the blob."

Otter nodded in agreement. "And this is the edge closest to the cottages, so…."

Atim rubbed his shoulder. "We probably moved the edge of that pile four feet back before we found the hole."

"That means…I would put it right about here." Otter pointed to a spot on the screen.

With a click, Denice added a green dot to the map right under Otter's finger.

The Chief smiled. "I'm sure that will help us in the future. Now that you've done the hard work, I'll have to look for it myself when I take my grandkids swimming in the summer."

The Muskrats smiled at each other.

Sam raised a hand. "So, the red lines…what are they?"

The Chief shook her head. "Those are the land claims we're still arguing over and negotiating for. Back in the Indian agent days, several land deals were made that were not very good for the people of Windy Lake, so we're looking at those. For some of them, the government will negotiate. For others, we may have to go to court."

Atim scratched his head. "Why do we have to fight for land that was ours in the first place?"

Denice sighed. "Reserves are not even our land. A reserve is Crown land that is held 'in reserve' for the use of First Nations people."

Chickadee's eyebrows scrunched together. "What's Crown land?"

The Chief turned to Chickadee. "It's government land. Land that Canada says it owns. Canadians saw the treaties as the First Nations ceding and surrendering all their lands. First Nations saw the making of treaty as the sharing of the land for the mutual and equal benefit of all."

Denice waved a hand in disgust. "There was a lot of fishy stuff going on. The First Nations did not understand English well. Some Elders say there was a lot of talk about Canadians wanting to grow crops and also wanting First

Nations to plant crops. They talked about wanting First Nations to *seed*—s-e-e-d—the land. At the same time, they talked about wanting the First Nations to cede—c-e-d-e—the land, which means to give it up. *Cede* and *seed*? They sound the same. Who knows if the First Nations really understood what they were agreeing to?"

It was Sam's turn to look confused. "So, what happens if we win a land claim for the bits in red? Does that land become First Nation land?"

The Chief shook her head. "No. If we win the land claim, a loss-of-use study will be done. A study that looks at how much money the First Nation could have made from the land if it had not been wrongfully taken. That amount would then be where the negotiations with Canada start."

Sam's lips tightened. "But we don't get the land back?"

"Nope," Denice answered. "Canada takes the way that's easiest for Canadian politicians, and there's Canadians living on that land."

Otter was studying one of the red areas on the map. "It looks like this land claim area is half full of King's Lumber Yard, and the big trucks and garages for his construction company."

The Chief nodded. "Yes. So, imagine what would happen if the government had to go to Mr. King and tell him they wanted his land and he had to move all his stuff. Mr. King wouldn't like that. He'd probably get angry and go to other Canadians, maybe his employees and neighbors, and ask them to vote out any politicians who were part of making the decision. Most Canadians think owning private property is one of their highest individual rights. Politically, resolving land claims can be a huge hot potato."

Denice scoffed. "Ask any Canadian whose lands have been taken by the government in order to build a highway or a mine, whether the government considers the whole country as owned by a Canadian collective!!"

The Chief's eyes twinkled when she looked back at Chickadee. "Your older cousin is passionate about injustice. She reminds me of me when I was young."

Denice's eyes got wide, and she straightened up in her seat. Her mouth opened to say something, but nothing came out.

The Chief continued. "When I was a young woman, I started the same way, working for Chief and Council. At that time, Windy Lake was negotiating a land claim, and I heard a young Canadian negotiator ask his mentor 'Why do they always ask for money?' And the older negotiator told him the truth. He said, 'It's all we offer.' You see, Canada doesn't offer anything except money because giving the land back is too much trouble politically. The Canadian system uses money to evaluate everything: services, products, human effort, time, and land."

Denice shook her head, angrily. "That's right! Canadians shouldn't blame First Nations for Canadian culture.

It's *their* culture that is obsessed with money. We'd be happy with the land back. We don't really care how many Canadian politicians get voted out. Instead, they give us money, and we must find land that Canadians are willing to sell."

The Chief nodded. "Settling land claims is not just important to resolve past injustices, it is important for the future, too. It is through the land that most Canadian towns fund themselves. Municipalities charge taxes, tariffs, and fees for citizens to access the land or the resources within that land, such as gravel to make roads and cement. So, First Nations having access to more land means they would be more self-sufficient."

Suddenly, Denice's keyboard clicked loudly as her fingers began to tap. A map of Canada spread across the projector screen. "And do you know what? If you put all the reserve lands from every First Nation across Canada together, they would be just a little larger than Vancouver Island in size!"

Otter stood back. He stretched his arms across the whole country, then took just two fingers to measure the length of Vancouver Island on the screen. "I don't think First Nations would give up all this for such a little bit."

Denice pursed her lips. "They didn't. Nobody would make that trade. As for what the Chief said about creating self-sufficiency from the land, that small area of reserve land is divided into six hundred and forty First Nation communities scattered across the country!"

Sam snapped his fingers. "So, with such a small amount of land for each community, the First Nations would never be able to be self-sufficient!"

The Chief pointed at Sam. "You got it. Today's Canadians say they want First Nations to be self-sufficient, but a proper land base is crucial for that."

Chickadee crossed her arms. "So, it seems even more important that we get to keep the land the cottages are on."

Playfully, Denice slapped her little cousin on the shoulder. "You got that right. That's why it is so important we find that pin."

"The cottages and the land they're on," the Chief continued, "would be a long-term, land-based gain that would help the Windy Lake First Nation to become more self-sufficient. It is very disappointing that so many years ago, the Indian Agents didn't really have the concerns of the communities they governed as a priority."

Otter stopped studying the map, turned, and leaned against the table. "It's like Chickadee always says. You need flour to make bannock. Well, we need more information about that pin to make our claim stick."

Atim nodded. "We've heard a bunch of rumors and stories. To hear Mavis tell it, the pin was a golden treasure stolen by 'Canadiana' Jones."

Sam chuckled. "Well, not quite that bad. But have you heard anything…official?"

The Chief thought for a few seconds. "Interestingly enough, we did hear some stuff. The RCMP invited us to look at a file. It was very old, and the case had been closed, so they didn't mind showing us what they had. But it was awfully vague. I'm not sure how much help it would be."

Denice scoffed. "I got the feeling that Mr. Scott is not the RCMP's favorite person."

Chickadee shook her head. "How could they close the case if the pin wasn't found?"

The Chief looked at her. "To be honest, the pin wasn't even mentioned in the file. The case they showed us was about the only break-in that involved the Factory Hall around the time the pin went missing."

Denice clicked her keyboard a few more times, and a picture of the Factory Hall's lobby filled the screen. "That case was actually about the old dress in the display cabinet." The mouse cursor circled the dress in the photo.

Chickadee leaned forward, her eyes wide open. "The plaques about the dress say the governor gave it to the most beautiful girl in the area for the very first Spring Feast held at Factory Hall."

Denice shook her head. "Yeah, well, someone stole it. But when the thief was found, the case was dropped with no charges laid. Apparently, it was at the request of everyone involved, but there were no names listed."

Sam pinched his chin. "Wow! Someone was trying to cover something up."

The Chief took a deep breath. "There was a line that said *her* family returned the dress. But no names."

Chickadee was surprised. "A girl!" she exclaimed.

Otter spoke thoughtfully, "A girl whose family could keep her name off the record."

Sam pointed a finger at his cousin. "That's right, Otter! They must have been an important family to be able to protect their daughter."

The Chief stared off into the distance as she searched her memory. "I wasn't born back then, but your grandpa would have been in his early twenties by that time, if my math is right. He might remember a girl that age in town...."

Just then, the Chief's mobile phone rang. Taking it out of her pocket, she apologized to Denice and the Muskrats for leaving. She answered the call as she walked out.

When she was gone, Atim blurted, "One of the rumors we heard was that Hayter Scott took the pin, and that Grandpa was friends with him when they were young."

Denice slapped her keyboard. "I bet Hayter stole it for his dad. He's the Indian Agent who set up the bad deal for the First Nation. Did you ask Grandpa about it?"

The Muskrats looked at each other.

"We tried to speak to him," Sam said.

"It didn't go too well," Otter added.

Chickadee reminded Denice that Grandpa hadn't spoken up at the meeting. Then she told her the story the aunties had discussed at bingo, about Grandpa liking a French-Canadian girl when he was young. Finally, she described what had happened that morning.

Denice took in all the new information. "You guys have been pretty busy!"

"Yeah," said Atim. "But we probably won't be asking Grandpa anything else about this."

Sam waggled his head. "Not until we gather more information, at least. Do you know of anyone else we could ask?"

Denice chuckled. "Well, you could go see Great-Uncle Ezekiel…if you dare. He should be getting ready to leave the trapping shack for the fishing cabin."

Otter was suddenly excited. "We could borrow Grandpa's canoe and be at Grandpa Zeke's trapping shack in a few hours."

The other Muskrats looked unconvinced. The Muskrats' great-uncle, or Grandpa Zeke as they called him, was the oldest of all their grandfather's brothers and commanded a lot of respect. He rarely came out of the bush, and in the solitude of the forest, he had grown a little crusty.

Sam was skeptical. "Do you really think he would help us?"

Denice nodded. "If you take the time to go out there, I'm sure he'll tell you something. He's the oldest, so he probably has memories of those days. He'll make you work for that info, of course."

With quick good-byes, the Muskrat left and headed for Grandpa's canoe.

CHAPTER 10

Burnt Out!

As soon as the Muskrats cleared the end of the bay, they knew something was wrong. The smell of burned wood and plastic was heavy in the air.

Otter was at the rudder, guiding the canoe and its little motor into the shoreline of sand and gravel. He answered the question nobody had wanted to ask. "You can't see Grandpa Zeke's cabin from the lake. You need to walk in a ways."

Once out of the canoe, the sleuths made their way up the slanted embankment. They found the well-used trail at the top and ran down it toward the trapping cabin. The smell of charred wood became heavier and heavier.

Chickadee had been leading, but before they went over the last rise of land, she stopped and held a hand to her lips. "Oh! My goodness, I hope he's okay."

Otter stepped around her. "We have to check!"

At the top of the little hill, the Muskrats gasped. In the midst of the clearing, Grandpa Ezekiel's trapping cabin was a blackened pile. One corner of the building stood defiantly, still supporting a small section of roof that poked toward the sky. Flattened layers of burned plywood and other materials made up the majority of the heap.

Chickadee stopped. Her eyes filled with tears as she shivered with the frightfulness of her thoughts. "Is he…?"

Atim, Sam, and Otter walked around the former cabin. The interior had burned until the whole building had collapsed in on itself, but the layers of sheet wood, still damp from the wetness of spring, had only burned on the edges and surface. A few busted traps, a bent frying pan, a broken axe handle, and the piles of odds and ends that result from a long-running camp were scattered here and there.

Atim took out their phone and started taking pictures.

Sam whispered, "I don't see any…bones."

Otter shook his head. "I don't see his boat, either. If he was still here, his boat would be in the bay."

Chickadee heaved a huge sigh. "Yes, of course. You're right. Thank you, Otter."

Atim walked over and gave her a hug.

"But someone other than Grandpa Zeke was here." Otter pointed at the ground.

The Muskrats gathered around him. The damp ground was marked with footprints and tire tracks.

Sam knelt down to get a closer look. "All-terrain vehicle tracks. A four-wheeler?"

Otter shook his head and pointed out another set of long depressions in the ground. "*Two* four-wheelers."

Atim studied the ground on the other side of the ruins. "There are some footprints over here."

The other detectives joined him. Otter stooped down to get a closer look. "These look like brand-new boots."

Atim arched an eyebrow. "Kind of looks like the tracks from Uncle Levi's police boots."

Otter nodded. "Yeah, hey?"

Chickadee was searching through the trees, her face full of worry. "What do we do now? I want to find him."

Otter closed his eyes in thought before he spoke. "Knowing Grandpa Zeke, if he wasn't hurt, he'd just pack up and go to his next camp."

"So, back to the canoe then?" Sam asked.

Otter hesitated. "If we go, we'll probably have stay out there. Grandpa doesn't let me use the canoe after dark."

Chickadee grabbed Otter's sleeve and tugged him along for a few steps toward the shore. "If we have to stay at Grandpa Zeke's shack, we will. After seeing his burned cabin, we can't just leave without making sure he's okay."

Sam frowned. "We could go back to town. Tell my mom what we saw here."

Otter snickered. "Grandpa Zeke would skin us alive if a search party showed up at his shack while he was sitting there listening to the radio."

Atim pulled out the Muskrats' Horn. "I have one bar. Could maybe get a text through."

Sam smiled. "Good idea, big bro. Let Mom know we're heading out to Grandpa Zeke's fishing cabin."

Atim threw a thumb over his shoulder. "Should I tell her about that?"

Otter shook his head. "That would get a search party started. He's probably at his fishing camp."

Reluctantly, Samuel agreed. "We'll check out the camp first. If there is something wrong, we'll try to come back to this one and send another text. Cool?"

"Cool," the Muskrats agreed.

Atim's thumbs danced as he texted his mother that the Muskrats were heading to the family's fishing camp to see Grandpa Zeke, and they weren't sure they'd be home before morning. He pressed send and then looked worried.

Sam noticed. "What now?"

Atim shrugged. "We're going to get in trouble, aren't we?"

Sam gave his brother's shoulder a squeeze. "Did you get a return text?"

After a quick glance at the phone, Atim shook his head.

Otter turned to his cousins. "If we leave now, there's a chance we can get back before dark. If we stay to wait for a text, that may have not got through, we're sleeping out here."

With that, the Muskrats hurried back down the to shore and scrambled into their vessel. It was a long way to the next camp, and the added journey almost guaranteed they'd be staying with Grandpa Zeke for the night.

As Atim pushed them off the shore into deeper water, he looked across the lake. "Good thing the weather is clear."

Once they were pointed in the right direction, Otter turned up their little outboard motor to full speed. The engine's little *putt-putt-putts* came at a clipped pace.

CHAPTER 11

Friendly Fire

It was late afternoon by the time the Muskrats pulled into shore and were back on land. They all stretched and rubbed their tired muscles and bones, achy from a long ride and the jarring of waves that arose with the wind.

Chickadee scanned the shore. Her voice quivered when she spoke. "I don't see a boat! Maybe he's not here!"

Otter pointed at a scar in the gravel, sand, and dirt of the shoreline. "Wait before you get upset and take a look at that. He may have pulled his boat out of the water and into the bush!"

Atim shook his head. "That's weird. Why would he do that?"

Sam looked confused. "It's a lot of work. But Grandpa Zeke wouldn't do something like that for no reason."

Chickadee waved the boys up the shore. "Let's go find him!"

Once into the bush, the Muskrats soon came across Grandpa Zeke's boat. They all sighed with relief. A few yards along the way to the cabin, the Muskrats could smell woodsmoke.

They jogged down the forest trail and quickly came to the multi-colored fishing cabin. Its outer walls were made of slabs of scrap wood hauled to the location through numerous boat trips. Each scrap of plywood was painted a different color, from forest green, to faded yellow, to royal purple, to functional blue. Small, four-paned windows faced each direction except north. Woodsmoke escaped from a tin chimney that stuck out of a roof hugged by curled red and black shingles.

The cabin door opened with a creak. Having heard their footsteps, Grandpa Zeke's eyes pierced theirs as they stepped through the doorway. He waited at a small kitchen table, a well-used mug of tea in his hands. His grudging smile was held in reserve until he saw who had come to visit.

Chickadee launched herself at her Elder as soon as she saw him. Just in time, he pulled his tea out of the way to miss being spilled by her hug. "Oh, Grandpa Zeke! We were so worried about you!"

The male Muskrats nodded, as they gathered around the old man. Grandpa Ezekiel was older than their own grandfather but was larger and rougher looking. His grip was like a vice, his hands coarse and calloused. His silver hair had been cut but was in need of a clipping. His gray bush jacket and khaki-colored pants were both made of thick canvas.

Slightly chagrined, their Elder gently pulled Chickadee's arms from around his neck. "I'm okay, my girl. So? You must have seen what they did to the trapping cabin."

The Muskrats nodded. Chickadee took up a seat beside her Elder, holding his hand.

Atim pressed a hand against his heart. "We thought you might be burned!"

Sam shook his head. "Your cabin looked like a pile of extra crispy lasagna, all collapsed in on itself."

"Who do you think torched it?" Otter asked.

Grandpa Zeke suddenly stood. "Let's go outside. I can't talk about this in here." The old man moved like a cougar, fast and quiet. The Muskrats tumbled out the door behind him.

While the family called it Grandpa Zeke's fishing cabin, the whole family used it. The old man did fish the lake from out of the shack, but really, its location had been chosen due to a nearby creek that teemed with spawning suckerfish in the early spring. The fish were full of bones, but the family came together every year to catch, clean, and can them. The process of canning softened the boney bits and left the fish meat soft and tasty. Grandpa Zeke always showed up at the camps early to prepare them for the family to come. Today, a silky wind carried the cabin's woodsmoke and the scent of pine sap through the trees.

Agitated, their Elder paced as he spoke. "I figure it was those conservation officers. They've been bugging me to tear down that cabin for years. They say it was put up without a building permit. Can you imagine?"

Atim lifted his shoulders, confused. "But it's out in the bush, in the middle of nowhere!"

Grandpa Ezekiel, still pacing, pointed at his grand-nephew. "Exactly, it has nothing to do with building permits or safety. They just don't want us using our traditional lands unless they're on-reserve. They want to enforce the idea that it is their land now. Canada ain't sharing it. That's why I pulled up my boat. I don't want to make it easy for them to find this cabin."

Chickadee shook her head. "The Chief told us that the treaties were about sharing the land, not giving it away."

Their Elder stopped and sighed. "Our family has been on these lands for generations. They say the Cree didn't have ownership of land. Well, that's just nonsense. There were many fights between First Nations over borders. And within Nations, if people took care of a piece of land, if they removed the dead wood and trees, spread the medicines where they could grow, took good care managing the animals and plants there—if they were really stewards of that bit of Mother Earth—then the community at-large would recognize those people as being in charge of that land. We may not have paid cash for our lands, but we worked to earn the right to care for them."

"I can't believe it was conservation officers!" Sam said.

Grandpa Zeke stopped and shook a finger at Sam. "I took the boat into town this morning. They saw me at the gas station. They had their ATVs on a trailer behind that government truck. I bet they took off as soon as they saw me, drove up as close as they could, and then used their four-wheelers the rest of the way. They knew I wouldn't let them burn my shack if I was there!"

Atim was angry. "The whole thing is outrageous!"

Sam gave a slight shrug. "Canada says we seeded the land. Oops! I mean, ceded—with a *c*—the land. What that really means is that their law always comes first."

Grandpa Zeke walked to the nearby firepit, knelt, and began to make a fire. "How can we live our lives our way without any land to stand on? They say we didn't *use* the land! City people say whole areas of lands are 'unusable,' but we see them as full of good resources, food, and medicines. Us Indians were spread across the land much more than we are now, and we took care of it."

Chickadee was collecting little sticks from the ground to serve as kindling for the fire. The brothers began to help her.

For a moment, Otter watched them, wondering how many forests and lands were tended, in part, by children just gathering dead wood for a campfire. "Grandpa says that's one of the reasons there are so many wildfires now. Nobody takes care of the bush."

Grandpa Zeke chuckled. "Well! If that's what my little brother says, it must be so."

The Muskrats giggled at the thought of their grandfather being someone's little brother. The tension that had filled the air surrounding the discussion of the burned cabin evaporated with the laughter.

Seeing the smiles on the Muskrats' faces, Grandpa Ezekiel chuckled himself, as he lit a match and held it to the kindling in the firepit. "Sorry for being so mad. You're the first people I could tell. I liked that little shack. We built it with my father when we were young. We brought in some of the original wood by dogsled."

Chickadee dropped another armful of small sticks beside her great-uncle. "We've been keeping that land clean for generations. Hey, Grandpa Z?"

The old man moved to sit on a stump of wood. He sighed and nodded his head. "It'll be up to you guys and your cousins to make the next cabin and take care of the lands we use."

Chickadee sighed. "I don't like it when Elders talk about not being here."

Grandpa Zeke laughed and gave Chickadee's shoulder a squeeze. "I'm still here, and not about to go anywhere, my girl. Soon it will be your time to be the hands of the family and do the work to keep us all going. And then, I can just sit back and be the old guy who remembers." With this last bit, he put his hands behind his head and pretended to lean back on an imaginary lounge chair, almost falling off his stump in the process.

The kids laughed as he righted himself.

Chuckling, he yelled, "Don't laugh at your Elders!" That made them all laugh harder.

When the hilarity puttered to a stop, Grandpa Zeke sighed happily. "Well, I imagine the Mighty Muskrats didn't come to visit me for nothing. I've been selfish. What can I do for you?"

The rest of the Muskrats let Sam fill their Elder in on the case. Dropping his load of sticks by the fire, he sat down on a stump and scratched the back of his head before he spoke. "We're looking for that surveyor's pin, stolen from the Factory Hall, that used to show where the border of the reserve land was."

Their Elder frowned and looked at the ground. "You know, I do remember the Factory Hall was broken into back then. But the hoopla about it died out pretty quick, if I remember correctly. Didn't hear much about it after that."

Atim spoke next. "We've heard a bunch of rumors, but we don't know what is true. Do you remember anything else about that time?"

Grandpa Zeke stared off into the universe as he traveled back in his memories. Suddenly, he clapped his hands three times. "*Boom! Boom! Boom!*" Then he shook his head. "That's what I remember! They were blasting for the dam. I got a job. The whole town vibrated from the blasts but also with all the young Canadians from down south coming up. *Everything* was changing."

Otter moved closer to the fire as it took better hold of the tinder. "What job did you get?"

Grandpa Ezekiel looked over at him. "I worked for the mining company back then, not at the mine, but unloading stuff from the docks. The mining company promised everybody they would update the area. We got stop signs for the first time. The Co-op got a walk-in fridge. I think the hardest thing we unloaded was this great big furnace for the Factory Hall."

Sam pointed at his great-uncle. "Mr. Dave told us about that. He showed us the Octopus!"

Grandpa Zeke slapped his knee, happily surprised. "He showed you that old relic? Yeah, they couldn't take that monster out, but they put in the new one we unloaded. Big and heavy, but still smaller than the Octopus. That original one was built right into the building, even its pipes were. They had to make new vents for the smaller furnace. Luckily, Mr. Dave's father was good at woodwork. He removed the old, fancy, cast-iron covers, put them over the new vents, and covered up the old holes. Most people don't know the Octopus is even down there."

Shyly, Chickadee turned to their Elder. "We heard Grandpa was friends with Hayter Scott back then. Maybe even liked a French girl."

Grandpa Zeke snorted and slapped his knee. "I ain't walking that trail! If you Muskrats want to know about my little brother's love life, you better ask him about it. Or…

you could ask…no, she doesn't need that." Grandpa Zeke slapped his knee. "You'll have to go to your Grandpa," he said, ending the subject.

They sat in silence for a while. There seemed to be no point in telling Grandpa Zeke that they had already tried speaking to their grandfather.

Atim looked at the sky. "Sun is a few hours away from going down."

Otter looked up too. "It's still spring. If we left right now, it would be dark by the time we got back."

Atim looked pained. "We're going to get in trouble."

Sam reached over and tugged on his brother's jacket. "We sent a text from the other camp. They'll know we're here."

Chickadee took a deep breath. "I bet my parents are wondering where I am, right now."

Otter shook his head. "I think we'd get in more trouble if we showed up in the boat after dark."

Grandpa Ezekiel listened to the young sleuths as they spoke. When they stopped, he pointed at Atim and then at the cabin. "There's a blue-and-white box on top of the fridge in there. Bring it here."

Atim raced off on the errand.

Grandpa Zeke wasn't finished. He motioned to Otter and then the cabin. "There's some wieners in that fridge and buns. Bring them there…." He pointed to a battered picnic table nearby. Then he motioned at Chickadee and

Sam. "You two, there's some willows over there, go cut some sticks." The rest of the Muskrats scattered as they went about their mission.

Atim brought back the box on a run. The Elder took it, placed it on his knee, and sent Atim back into the cabin to mix some juice crystals with water and bring back some cups and ketchup.

When the Muskrats all returned, he lifted up the box. "My daughters gave me this for my birthday, but I've never even put the batteries in." He handed the package to Atim.

Opening the lid, Atim smiled. "A satellite phone! We won't get in trouble after all!"

CHAPTER 12

A Prisoner to Perspective

The next morning, as the Muskrats canoed up to Windy Lake, Atim and Sam could see their mother's van waiting on the shore.

Atim leaned over to his little brother and, shouting to be heard above the canoe's motor, said, "Uh-oh."

Sam smiled and waved off the concern.

When the Muskrats pulled up in the boat, the boys' mother waved to them excitedly. "Hey, you kids. Hurry up! I need some help with the groceries." She opened the large side door to the van, and they all climbed in.

Atim looked around. "Where are the groceries?"

His mother snorted. "Haven't picked them up yet." She looked at them in the rearview mirror. "Did Grandpa Zeke feed you?"

Atim moaned. "He fed us breakfast, but that was more than three hours ago!"

Sam yelled with fake concern. "He's fading fast Mom! We have to get him to the store!"

The boys' mother smiled as she yelled back. "We're going to the store! Hang in there, boy!"

Chickadee leaned forward from the backseat. "Yay! I wanted to go to the Co-op!"

Her auntie shook her head. "We're going to the Crossroads. I need the better stuff. I'm making fancy food for the Spring Feast. Nothing frozen." With that, she turned the van toward the Canadian side of Windy Lake.

The Crossroads was like most intersections in Windy Lake, a meeting of gravel roads. However, at this one sat a bright yellow, two-story building with a big, hand-painted sign proclaiming it as the Lacroix General Store. The old building was really a large old house, with the general store and its storage room on the first floor and office and living quarters on the top floor. Both the building and the Lacroix family had been in the area since the fur trade. The current keeper of the store, Ms. Lacroix, was the last of her kin.

Chickadee studied the big sign once she stepped out of the van. "It's weird that we hardly ever come to this store."

Her auntie closed the van door and checked to make sure she had her wallet with her. "You know…your grandmother and grandfather never came here, so we rarely come. It's funny how people copy their parents that way."

The bell above the door tinkled as they entered the store.

The dim lighting inside dampened the color of the packaged products lining the shelves. The bright yellow of the storefront had never stepped inside. There didn't seem to be any other customers. The cashier was a bored, blonde teenager in a blue apron. She perked up and smiled as they entered.

Always friendly, Chickadee knew the teenager at the till and skipped up to speak with her.

Atim and Sam's mother grabbed a cart from the few lined up by the door and headed into the store.

Atim shivered. "The air feels cold and old in here."

Looking around as he followed his auntie, Otter was distracted as he spoke. "Yeah, but not like the 'cheap plywood of the Co-op store' old. More like the 'clammy skin of time and boards beaten smooth' old."

His cousins nodded, not at all shocked that Otter had said something unexpected.

Sam smiled and whispered, "Nailed it."

Atim tugged his mother's sleeve. "Do you mind if we go check out what they have in the cereal aisle?"

She shook her head as she studied a box of biscuits.

The boys took off, joking and jostling, as they looked for the selection of sugar breakfasts. They were happy to find a much larger choice than what was at the Co-op.

Atim's voice was strained as he spoke. "I can't believe how many of these I've never tasted!"

Sam picked up a bright red box. "I thought you could only get this stuff in the city!"

Otter chuckled. "Grandpa only buys big bags of puffed wheat. He says it's good stuff because we can put it in a pillowcase and use it when we sleep, too. He thinks that's funny."

Atim held up a box with a cartoon character on it. "Look at this! *Ya-ba-daba-diabetes!*"

His brother and cousin laughed.

As the boys continued to look over the cereal, Otter heard a board creak. Turning, he saw a gray-haired lady in a flowered dress, leaning forward just enough that she could watch them from the end of the aisle. When she saw Otter had noticed her, she ducked out of sight. Otter looked away slightly but kept the end of the aisle in the corner of his eye.

Sam nudged his cousin's arm, box in hand. "Check out this one...." Realizing Otter was distracted, he nudged his cousin again. "What's up?"

Otter lip-pointed toward the old woman. "We're being watched."

Sam looked just in time to catch the lady leaning forward to see what the boys were doing. He pulled on his brother's jacket. "Hey Atim, let's go see if they have anything that looks like a toy section," he said in a louder-than-normal voice.

Atim put the box down, his cereal dreams stowed away for future reference. The boys walked down the way they had come and then searched the other aisles. Finding one with a small assortment of toys and games, the boys began to check out options.

Atim pointed to one shelf. "Going to be warm enough for squirt guns soon."

Otter kept an eye on the end of the row. The floor-boards creaked just before the old lady peeked around the corner again. He nudged Sam.

Sam quickly turned to the old lady. "Can we help you?"

The reply was the creak of boards as the woman retreated.

Sam turned to Otter, his eyebrows furrowed in consternation. "Who was that?"

Otter closed an eye as he pondered. "Ms. Lacroix, I bet."

Atim stopped studying the toys. "What's going on?"

At that moment, Chickadee walked up. "What are you two doing? Your mom is at the cashier."

Otter and Sam stepped closer. "There was an old woman watching us."

Chickadee snorted. "Yeah. Probably Ms. Lacroix. She's one of the reasons a lot of people from the rez don't come here. They say she watches us pretty closely."

Otter snickered. "We didn't even get a good look at her." He covered one side of his face. "Just one eye poking around the corner."

Atim's lips tightened. "Wait. You mean she thought we might be stealing? That's not cool."

The other Muskrats shrugged as if to say, *That's just the way it is.*

Sam tugged at the end of his brother's braided pony-tail. "I think you better get used to it, especially if we move back to the city after high school."

Chickadee sighed, then nodded her head toward the front of the store. "Come on. Your mom will be waiting."

When they got to the cashier, Chickadee said good-bye to the girl at the till. The boys loaded the recycled shopping bags that Atim and Sam's mother pulled out of a purse one size short of needing wheels. Once their bags were full, the boys picked them up and waddled out of the store.

Once his load was piled in the back of the van, Sam glanced back at the store. "I think Ms. Lacroix was watching us in there."

His mother scoffed. "I have no doubt she was. Why do you think I brought you? I hate it when that old woman follows me around. It's the second reason I hardly ever shop here."

Sam gave his mom's arm a playful slap. "You mean… you were using us as decoys?"

His mother smiled knowingly, then found the van keys in the bottom of her purse. With the groceries loaded, they all got into the vehicle.

She waved at the building in front of them. "This place is more expensive than the Co-op, too. That's the third reason I usually don't come here."

Atim looked over at his mother. "It's not a good feeling when someone treats you like you're going to steal something."

His mom gave him a sympathetic smile and squeezed his arm. "Unfortunately, it happens."

Chickadee looked out the window. "The cashier says the old lady is scared, like, all the time. She says Ms. Lacroix never leaves the store and hardly ever comes down from her living quarters upstairs."

Otter frowned. "That's sad. Imagine feeling like you're surrounded by people you're scared of."

His auntie looked at him in the rearview mirror. "That's good to try to understand her, Otter. Now that I think of it, I have never seen Ms. Lacroix around town. I guess her fear is genuine, but honestly, I don't know anybody who would want to hurt Ms. Lacroix. Or steal from her, for that matter."

Atim's shoulders slumped. "I was mad at her, but now…I'm sad for her."

Sam looked back at the building as the van pulled away. "She's made that house a prison. It has everything she needs, so she never has to leave."

Atim shook his head. "The only bars are chocolate bars."

Chickadee leaned forward and gave Atim a punch on the arm. "Don't make fun of that old lady."

Atim pulled back in shock. "I wasn't. Just saying."

"He can't help it," Sam said. "When he goes deep, he hits his stomach."

Their driver sighed. "Okay. That's enough Muskrats for me. Where am I dropping you boneheads off?"

CHAPTER 13

Fort Farts

Exasperated, Samuel gestured with his arms as he paced down the length of the Mighty Muskrats' school-bus fort. "We can't take on the case of the sad, old woman. We have to find that pin!"

Arms crossed, Chickadee sat on the low couch, her black hair spread out over her favorite hoodie, legs stretched out ridged, like she was putting on the brakes. "I'm going to help Ms. Lacroix. She can't spend the last of her days in that gloomy…storehouse."

Sitting on the weight bench recycled from the junk-yard outside, Atim curled a barbell as he listened to the debate.

Seemingly oblivious to the conversation, Otter quietly strummed a battered guitar.

Sam stopped and shook his head. "First things first. If we started something, we have to finish it."

Chickadee huffed. "I'm smart enough to chew gum and walk at the same time. I don't even know what I'm going to do for Ms. Lacroix. I just know I'm going to do *something*. So...settle down."

Not looking at his cousin, Sam walked to the small kitchen table. A sound like a robot's fart ripped through the bus as he pulled out the chair and its legs scraped across the metal floor. Still unsmiling, Samuel sat with his arms crossed and his back straight. "Well, it better not interfere with the Case of the Pilfered Pin."

Chickadee was annoyed enough not to react to the fart sound, either. She held up a finger. "You can't tell me...."

Otter's guitar went *ba-TWANG!!* And then he thumped its body. He had the attention of all the Muskrats.

"Remember Chickadee said that Elder at bingo told the aunties that Grandpa liked a French girl?"

His cousins nodded.

"Remember when the Chief told us that there was no file on the missing pin? Back then, nobody seemed to notice it had disappeared, I guess. But there *was* a file on a girl who tried to steal the beautiful dress!"

Sam pinched his chin thoughtfully. "Yeah. And the file was closed with no charges laid. Could be a sign of a powerful family."

Otter continued to strum as he spoke. "And Grandpa Zeke, he said, 'No, she doesn't need that,' just after Chickadee asked him about a French Canadian girl."

Chickadee sat up straight on the couch. "Hey, that's right. What are you thinking, Otter?"

"Well, Lacroix is a French name, right?" he said.

Sam snapped his fingers. "Wow! Yes! And Ms. Lacroix and Grandpa were about the same age—early twenties—around the time of the break-in and when the pin went missing."

Atim paused mid arm-curl. "So, you think Ms. Lacroix stole the dress or the pin?"

Otter put the guitar down. "I don't know. But people seem to think the two events are connected, or at least that they happened around the same time. Even the RCMP mentioned the dress break-in to the Chief and Council when they asked about the pin going missing."

Sam stood up and began to pace again. "But there's nothing connecting Ms. Lacroix to either event."

"Yeah, true," Otter admitted. "But her family was very influential in the area, she is French Canadian, and from what Grandpa Zeke almost kind of said, the girl that Grandpa may have liked is still available to answer questions, so she must be alive and close. Right?"

"Yeah, that all adds up," Sam said.

Chickadee held up a finger. "Wait. Why would a French Canadian twenty-something steal a Métis woman's dress?"

Otter shrugged. "I have no idea, but we have to start somewhere."

Sam stopped his pacing in front of Otter. "So, you think if we take the case of the sad, old lady, we might find out more about the pilfered pin?"

Otter smiled. "Sure."

Atim's barbell hit the steel floor with a bang. "Well, that's all I need to hear. What should we do next?"

Sam held out his hand to Chickadee. "I'm willing to combine the cases, if we can solve them both."

Chickadee ignored the outstretched hand and gave him a big hug. She pulled out a seat at the old kitchen table and looked at all her boys. "Okay, gather around. I think I know how we can do this."

CHAPTER 14

Dressing for Disaster?

"I think you're all crazy. This plan is more likely to explode in your faces than come out the way you want it." Denice shook her head at her little cousins.

Chickadee beamed up at her. "Oh, Denice. But just think how wonderful it would be if it worked out!"

Atim lifted an eyebrow. "I think it's only natural for people to believe their plan is going to work."

"Which is why a lot of people get disappointed," Sam observed.

Chickadee punched his bicep. "But we're going to *make* this work out, aren't we?"

Atim and Otter nodded enthusiastically. Sam nodded a little slower and rubbed his arm.

The Spring Feast was in full swing. People had already gone through the line and were sitting at tables eating. Beyond the dining area, a few rows of chairs guarded the empty stage on either side of a wide center aisle. A podium had been placed on one side, and behind it, a Canadian flag stood beside an eagle staff. Alone on the other side of the stage was the faded white dress from the display case in the lobby. The Factory Hall echoed with the sound of gossip and laughter as more families spilled in.

While the others stood and greeted guests, Atim sat at a table wiping moose meat gravy from the side of his mouth. "There is no meat better than moose meat," he declared.

Nobody disagreed.

Denice looked at her clipboard, then her watch. "We have to get the agenda started. Somebody go tell Grandpa that we'll be asking him to do the prayer soon."

"I can do that!" Chickadee skipped off, happy to engage one part of her plan.

Taking a few quick steps to keep up with her, Otter followed along. "Do you think she'll show up?"

Chickadee smiled at him. "I hope so. Denice sent her an official invite. So, why wouldn't she show?"

Otter shrugged. "The fact that she hardly ever leaves her house, maybe?"

Chickadee frowned and shrugged. "You know Windy Lake, maybe there was nothing interesting enough for her to leave, until tonight."

Otter gave his cousin a light punch in the shoulder. "Come on, Chickadee. What did you do?"

Chickadee did a slow blink and tried to look innocent. "Well…I did make a follow-up call after the invitation went out. When Ms. Lacroix said she wasn't sure if she was going to come, I just happened to mention that there were rumors about someone stealing the Métis dress a long time ago. And whoever stole that dress must have cared a lot about it to take it. Anyhow, I told her it had been all cleaned up and was looking great and that it would be on display at the Spring Feast."

Otter looked at her approvingly. "Reminding her of her old feelings just might get her to come. Good thinking." Otter lip-pointed toward the side of the room. And him?"

In a quiet corner, Hayter Scott was unloading a few display pieces from his jewelry store. His logo and phone number were displayed in gold letters on the ceiling banner, wall posters, and the tablecloth he had unfurled over a folding table.

Chickadee grinned at her cousin proudly. "I convinced Denice, and then she convinced her boss, that it would be nice to offer Mr. Scott an olive branch by giving him a chance to advertise his business at the Spring Feast. You know, it's for everyone in Windy Lake, not just the people from the rez. And he's sponsoring the event."

Their grandfather was sitting along the center aisle, a few rows from the front. He was laughing and talking with some Elders and several of the older aunties and uncles.

His hair was in a braid, and he wore a beaded, deerskin vest that still smelled of the woodsmoke their late grandmother had used to tan it. The beaded turquoise, green, and orange flower above his heart was their family crest.

Chickadee and Otter walked up, saw that their Elders noticed them, and waited until the last of their conversation rumbled to a stop.

After a moment or two, the Elders turned, and their grandfather smiled as he greeted them. "It is so good to see you, little ones. Is it time?"

Chickadee nodded politely at the other Elders before giving her grandfather a half-hug, while he continued to sit in the chair. "Almost ready, Grandpa? The emcee will tell you when it's time to come up."

The old man patted her arm. "I'll be ready, my girl. But I have to ask. Why is the old dress up there?"

Chickadee smiled. "We're honoring the lady that the dress was first given to. We did some research, and we think she would have been two hundred years old this year!"

Otter waggled his hand. "From what we read—well, Sam read—we may be off by a year or two either way, because the records weren't great back then."

The Elders laughed, nodding in agreement.

Grandpa turned his legs into the aisle, one hand on the back of the chair, the other on his walking stick, getting ready to rise. "Let's go now. It'll take me a while to get up there."

Waving good-bye to the other Elders, Chickadee and Otter led their grandfather toward the front of the stage.

Grandpa looked thoughtful as he scanned it. "It's good that you are honoring the history of that dress, but I'm sure you do not know it all. Not many do."

Chickadee smiled up at him. "That's why we had Denice send an official invite to Ms. Lacroix. Her family has been in this area for so long, we thought she would probably know something more about it."

Grandpa stopped. A worried look crossed his face as he turned to them. "Really?"

His grandchildren nodded.

Chickadee took his elbow and got him moving toward the stage again. "You've never spoken of her, Grandpa, and you've never taken us to her store, so we weren't certain if you knew her."

Grandpa tapped the hand holding his arm. "Of course I do, my girl. But I have not seen her in many, many years."

Chickadee squeezed his elbow. "It'll be good to see an old friend again, won't it?"

Grandpa didn't say a word. But Otter noticed he looked over his shoulder, back to where Hayter Scott was setting up his jewelry table.

When they got to the side of the stage, a few of the VIPs in front-row seats stood and greeted the Elder. Then Grandpa sat in the front-row chair closest to the stage stairs.

The emcee took to the stage a moment later and loudly welcomed everyone to the Spring Feast.

Chickadee and Otter hurried to the back of the room to help the guests.

Sam shook his head when they came up. "She's not here yet!"

Chickadee bit her lip thoughtfully. "Well, maybe this won't work. Maybe she won't come."

Ken, the emcee, was a well-known powwow caller from the area, who was rolling out all the same droll jokes. "I'm going to call up the Elder now to pray. Stand up, sit down if you want. This isn't church, so do what you like. No one is judging. Hey, Elder?"

Grandpa took the podium he was offered, as the emcee adjusted the mic closer to the old man's mouth. "Good evening, everyone. As Ken will tell you, back in the old days they lived in teepees and wigwams and I can't imagine everyone standing up in one of those, whenever someone acknowledged spirit. Do what you like, stand up or sit down. Go pee if you've had too much coffee and that is what your body is telling you to do. I'm going to pray now in my language."

With that, Grandpa took a step back from the podium and bowed his head. He began to pray in Cree. When he was done, he stepped toward the microphone again. "For those who do not understand my language, I will tell you what I said in my prayer. Ken inspired me to think of my Elders and how they used to pray. I remember how their prayers were almost songs. They spoke in this singsongy voice when they prayed. And they never asked for anything. They only gave thanks because they believed that everything a human needed to live a good life was already here...."

From where Grandpa was speaking, he could see the door to the lobby open. The evening sun was low enough that shards of sunlight shot through the lobby windows. This glow rushed into the main room as the door opened. It formed a halo around the person, their identity obscured by the light. But as the figure stepped forward, Grandpa realized he was looking at an old friend. Someone he hadn't seen in many, many years, someone he had cared about long before, and someone he hadn't expected to see.

Grandpa had to swallow the lump in his throat before he could speak again. "And so, in my prayer, I gave thanks. I gave thanks for my people here, but I also gave thanks for our good Canadian neighbors. I gave thanks for these lands that provide so much for us. I gave thanks for the minds we were given and how we can use our brains to overcome differences. And I gave thanks for our hearts and the knowledge that everyone hurts when a loved one dies...or their heart is broken." He paused for a moment, then looked up at the assembly and smiled. "And everyone likes good food and good friends. So maybe…*maybe* we can build an understanding from that." As he ended, he nodded at Ken and walked off the stage.

CHAPTER 15

Facing Fears

When the door opened as Grandpa spoke, Chickadee's excitement level hit the ceiling.

Otter shielded his eyes with his hand against the bright light. "Is it her?"

The door closed and the light lost its harsh edge. Left in the glow was an elderly woman in a fancy, flower-print dress. She looked like she'd stepped out of an old movie. Her hair was styled to perfection, her cheeks held the proper amount of rouge, her purse was a thing of beauty.

Denice spoke first. "Ms. Lacroix, thank you so much for accepting our invitation."

The old lady spoke hesitantly with a French accent. "I haven't left my home in a very long time, but I had to be here."

"Ms. Lacroix, let us help you to the seats by the stage," Chickadee said.

The storekeeper held out her wrinkled hand, and Sam stepped up quickly to take it. Ms. Lacroix leaned on him heavily and looked him in the eye. "Thank you. Lead the way, Monsieur."

Sam didn't see any of the distrust Ms. Lacroix had displayed in the store. He led her up the center aisle between the chairs.

"Give her the seat across the aisle from Grandpa," Chickadee whispered in Sam's ear. She then stepped in front of the pair, walking backward as she spoke. "Can you see what's on the stage, Ms. Lacroix?"

Looking up, the storekeeper saw the dress. She stopped. Sam could feel a tremble run through her body. She looked at Chickadee. "I haven't seen that in a very long time."

"We vacuumed the dust off it and aired it out before we put it up there."

Ms. Lacroix began to walk again and allowed herself to be guided to the chair Chickadee had picked for her. Once she was sitting, Chickadee pointed her out to the emcee, who gave Chickadee a thumbs-up.

Over the next half hour, politicians from both the Canadian and First Nation sides of Windy Lake stepped up to the podium and spoke about the importance of community and all the great work they were planning on doing in the not-too-distant future—if everything went according to plan.

At first, Grandpa didn't acknowledge Ms. Lacroix, stealing glances when he thought she wasn't looking. But eventually their eyes met, and Grandpa's crinkled as he nodded a greeting at her. Chickadee heard Ms. Lacroix gasp. And then the elderly lady turned to the front, patted her perfect hair, smoothed her clothes, and placed her purse on her lap.

Finally, the politicians rumbled to a stop, and Ken took the microphone again. "Ladies and gentlemen, you may be wondering why we have this dress up here tonight. Well, this is a special Spring Feast! We are honoring Sarah Beauvais, the Métis girl who wore this dress. This year would have been her two hundredth birthday, more or less! Now, there are many who say this dress represents the good relations between the Indigenous Peoples and Settlers in the Windy Lake area. But, you know what? Why hear her story from me? We have a special guest in the house. Chickadee, if you could help Ms. Lacroix onto the stage."

A murmur went through the crowd, as many people had never seen the storekeeper out of her home and workplace. Those at the back of the room stood to get a better view as Chickadee helped her up the steps to the stage.

Once she was at the podium, Ms. Lacroix turned to look at the dress for a long time. Then she straightened and seemed to cast off her frailty. "Sarah was a strong Métis woman...and she was my ancestor."

Another murmur flowed through the audience. For as long as the gathered adults could remember, the Lacroix family had been vehemently proud of being French—and *only* French.

"Yes, my family was Métis! But we hid those roots."

The crowd went silent.

"I'm an old woman now, so maybe it's time that I tell Sarah's story. *Our* story. You see, Sarah was the most beautiful young girl in the territory. Even though she was Métis, she was one of the few unmarried women invited to the first Spring Feast after the Factory Hall was built. With her father's permission, the governor gave her this dress that she wore to the feast."

The old lady turned to the dress and stared at it again.

"After the construction of the Factory Hall, other buildings, real homes, were built here in Windy Lake. With places where Canadians could settle, the fur traders left their First Nation wives and brought their European wives to the territory. And suddenly, Sarah wasn't invited to the feast anymore. As a Métis woman, she was not considered suitable company for European women."

Chickadee looked at Sam and her mouth opened, but nothing came out.

"For some reason, they didn't put that history in the display case," Sam whispered to her.

Ms. Lacroix look down to the front row of chairs and at Grandpa. She smiled at him as she spoke. "Now, I want to tell you about two old friends...."

The Muskrats looked at the back of the room and saw Mr. Scott standing behind his jewelry stand, rigid with attention.

"When I was a young woman, they were building the dam so the mine could grow. They wanted to attract a lot of young Canadians to town and make them feel welcome. So, they put things into the display case that indicated everything was fine here, that there were no problems between Canadians and the First Peoples who lived on these lands."

Ms. Lacroix laughed into the microphone with a strong chuckle followed by a girlish giggle. Then she looked down and composed herself. "I am sorry. It is not a funny thing, but the false story they were trying to sell to newcomers upset me. It made me angry because I knew the dress was given to Sarah, yes, but then she was rejected. Suddenly, she was treated as less than the European women who came later. I was hurt that her dress was being used to cover up the truth. So, I decided to take that dress. I convinced two of my good friends to help me, two young men."

She looked down at the Muskrats' grandfather again and smiled at him. "We only had the dress for a little while, before two of us got caught with it. And my father, he made sure that it was covered up. You know why? Because the friend I was caught with was a First Nation young man! And in those days, it wasn't proper for a young

Canadian girl to be in the company of an Indian. So, my father asked the authorities to drop all charges. That way, nobody would know that I was caught alone, talking with a young First Nation man. My father forbade me from speaking to my friend again. The dress went back into the case, and Sarah and her incomplete story were used once again. I am happy to be telling her true story now."

Ms. Lacroix blinked back a few tears. "You know, over the years, my father's thinking, my father's distrust, seeped into me. In the darkness of that store, I was filled with shadows. I stopped being a good neighbor, I stopped being a friend. And now, I want to change that." She nodded as though making a commitment to herself and to those listening.

She motioned with her hand, pointing out Chickadee and Denice to the crowd. "I must thank these young women for inviting me to speak for Sarah. Things weren't good between Canadians and First Nations when Sarah was young. They were still not good when I was young, but I see these young people, today's young people, and I think they are special. I hope the seed of a proper relationship between First Nations and Canadians has been planted here."

With that, she left the podium. Ken grabbed the microphone and asked everyone to give Ms. Lacroix a round of applause. The crowd heartily complied.

CHAPTER 16

Flames of Friendship

After a few more speakers and a flurry of bad jokes from Ken, the formalities and dinner came to a close.

As the people slowly left, Grandpa and Ms. Lacroix sat at a table at the back of the room drinking decaffeinated tea, due to the late hour. As they spoke, they had an audience of young sleuths waiting to ask them questions.

Grandpa's head was bent with sadness. "So much time has gone by without us speaking of what happened. Back then, I didn't want to cause trouble for you. And then I found the love of my life, and we started a family. Life... *time* just flows so fast when you're a parent."

Ms. Lacroix nodded. "Yes. And back then my father made me angry, but I loved him very much. I think that after he died, I became a reflection of him. I let his fears become my own. And I let that fear keep me away and apart from everyone. I didn't have to do that."

Grandpa smiled at the Muskrats. "Louise, Ms. Lacroix to you, was like Denice, back then. She asked questions about everything. She got me and…Hayter all fired up. We started to see the dress as being locked away in its own little prison."

"We have to save that dress!" Ms. Lacroix laughed out loud and tapped the table. "I remember saying that to both of you."

Sam couldn't hold himself back any longer. "What happened? What did you do?"

Ms. Lacroix smiled at him. "Oh! I needed help to get into the Factory Hall and move that display case away from the wall. Your Grandpa and Hayter helped me."

The Muskrats' eyes went wide.

Otter looked at his Grandpa. "Break and enter, Grandpa?"

Grandpa was about to speak, but Ms. Lacroix interjected. "Your grandfather and Hayter did trespass, but there was no breaking anything. And I took the dress."

Placing a hand on the table and tapping it to draw everyone's attention, Grandpa spoke in a sad, low voice. "I was a foolish young man. And I was punished! We were caught. Hayter got off without any consequences. But while Louise's father saved me from being charged, that RCMP sergeant made my life a nightmare until he finally moved away from Windy Lake."

Ms. Lacroix reached out and laid her hand on his. "I put you up to it, my friend. And my father didn't save you out of the goodness of his heart, he saved you because he didn't want word to spread that his daughter was found alone with an Indian."

Without thinking, Chickadee blurted out, "Were you boyfriend and girlfriend?"

The Elders pulled their hands back quickly.

Grandpa's eyes were stern as he shook his head. "No, we were just friends!"

The Muskrats giggled at their reaction.

Ms. Lacroix laughed. "A lot of girls had eyes for your grandpa back then. And Hayter!"

"Did I hear my name?" Mr. Scott had been putting away his jewelry but was now standing right beside their table!

The Muskrats gasped as they realized Mr. Scott had heard them talking.

Grandpa looked up at him. A balloon of tension suddenly inflated between the two men.

Otter whispered what was in his head. "Are they gonna fight?"

The two old men looked at the youngest of the Muskrats. Then they chuckled.

Grandpa spoke first. "No, little one. We never *wanted* to fight. We just did."

A smile grew on Mr. Scott's face. "Right. But I don't think you can say you didn't have a crush on Louise. We both did."

Ms. Lacroix looked surprised. "Really?"

Both men nodded.

Grandpa shook his head. "That's why we helped you. And while we were doing it, we found out we were both doing it for the same reason...to impress you."

Mr. Scott took a deep breath. "And once we had the dress—the way you thanked him—it was obvious you liked him more than me."

"And...is that why you became so angry?" Grandpa asked.

"Yes. Well, partially. My father found out I liked Louise, and he told me it would never work, because she was French and Catholic, and I was English and Protestant. And I didn't even go to Sunday school!"

Ms. Lacroix looked at the Muskrats' grandfather. "And *my* father told me he would strap me if he caught me talking to you. He never punished me, ever. But I knew he was serious when he told me to stay away from 'that Indian boy.' So, I did."

Grandpa smiled. "We all have much to regret. And so much time has passed. We should have had this talk a long time ago."

Atim's brow was furrowed. "So...you're both Canadians, but your parents were prejudiced against each other?"

Ms. Lacroix and Mr. Scott both nodded.

There was a short pause before Ms. Lacroix spoke. "When people hate, they look for difference. It doesn't matter what the difference is. Back then, the English looked down on the French because we were Catholics, not Protestant. And the French looked down on the English, too. But if it hadn't been for that, it would have been for something else."

Mr. Scott agreed. "Back then there was a ladder of prejudice. And it didn't matter who you were, people would put you on a rung and treat you how they defined you."

Otter shrugged. "Seems like it's still that way a lot of the time."

Samuel couldn't hold back his questions any longer. "So, what about the pilfered pin? Did you take the pin with the reserve boundaries etched on it?"

The three Elders shook their heads.

"It was still there when we left," Grandpa said.

Ms. Lacroix nodded. "We were there to save the dress, not to take the pin."

Mr. Scott smirked at Sam. "Like I said before, I know about as much as your Grandpa, and we didn't touch that pin!"

CHAPTER 17

Up in Arms!

"We've lost all our leads. This case is going nowhere!" Sam threw his hands up.

The day after the Spring Feast, the Mighty Muskrats gathered in their fort to end all forts.

Atim sat on his weight bench, staring at the floor, thinking hard. "Everyone says it was stolen, and all the possible suspects we had have been crossed off our list."

Sitting at the computer, Chickadee was searching for photos of surveyor pins. "We have to find something! There must be some clue as to how it disappeared."

Sam shook his head. "I guess we need to get out there and find more people who know what happened so long ago. Is there anything or anyone we missed?"

Sitting on the low couch against the wall of the school bus, Otter ventured a thought. "Not sure if it will help, but there was something that made me wonder."

"Anything could be a clue at this point," Atim told him.

"Well, remember when we were talking to Mr. Dave? When you told him we were looking for the pin, the first thing he said was that his dad hated that thing. I wonder why he hated it?"

Sam nodded vigorously. "Yes, now I remember that. I wonder why he hated an inanimate object."

Chickadee shut down the computer. "Mr. Dave is always at the Factory Hall. Why don't we go ask him?"

In a few moments, the young sleuths were walking down the road to the Factory Hall.

They arrived at their destination a short time later. The Factory Hall was empty, but it was unlocked. Atim pushed open one of the heavy doors and held it for the others. Once inside, they checked out the display case. The dress was back in its little glass room, but the card that had explained its history had been removed.

Chickadee touched the glass as she spoke. "Denice said she is going to write up Sarah's real history. It'll be better, I think. Sadder, for sure, but more truth to it."

Sam stood back from the display, pinching his chin. "What are we missing?"

Otter looked through the glass doors on both sides of the lobby. "The front doors were open, so Mr. Dave has to be around here somewhere."

Atim stuck his head into the main room. "He's not in here. Should I go around and find him?"

"I wouldn't bother," Otter said. "He's like Grandpa. I bet he's already heard us and is on his way."

Sure enough, Mr. Dave's soft baritone came from behind. "Can I help you?" None of the Muskrats had heard him walk up.

The young investigators turned.

Smiling after being startled, Sam nodded his hello. "Good to see you, Mr. Dave. I think Otter has a question for you."

"Yes," Otter said. "I was wondering…. When we were here before, you said your dad hated the surveyor's pin. Why?"

Mr. Dave chuckled. "He thought it was alive and had a mind of its own! He figured it didn't like being inside and was always trying to get away."

The Muskrats laughed.

Otter took off his baseball hat and scratched his head. "What do you mean? How was it alive?"

Mr. Dave rubbed the back of his neck and looked at the ground. "I remember my dad said he found it a few times, not in the display case, but down at the bottom of the stairs by the front doors. That's why he thought it was trying to get away."

Atim shook his head. "That's freaky! Maybe it was trying to get back to Picnic Creek Point."

Mr. Dave smirked. "Dad thought it was possessed."

Chickadee looked scared. "I would probably think the same thing!"

Sam took a deep breath. "You know, the edges of the head of the pin, as well as the pin's blunt end, were round. If something got it moving, it would roll in kind of a half circle."

Otter snapped his fingers. "Wasn't it put in there when they were making the dam and hydroelectricity station for the mine? Mr. Dave, didn't you say your mom's cupboards shook when the blasting was going on?"

A big smile crossed Atim's face. "Maybe it wasn't stolen! Maybe it left by itself! Could it be in the dirt outside?"

Mr. Dave shook his head. "We've fixed up the stairs and the parking lot since then. If it was found during construction, whoever found it probably didn't know what it was."

Sam pinched his chin. "When did you fix up the parking lot?"

Mr. Dave shrugged. "Long after the pin went missing. That construction couldn't have moved it."

Atim covered his eyes with his hands. "And even if it was found outside, the workers wouldn't have known what it was and would likely have trashed it."

Otter looked up at Mr. Dave. "Was there any construction going on around the time the pin went missing?"

Mr. Dave looked at the floor, going back in his memory. "Well, there was the furnace. The second one was installed around that time."

As Atim nodded his head, his braid, hanging over his shoulder, jumped. "Our Grandpa Zeke told us about that. He said he helped unload it."

Otter took a big breath, his eyes getting wider. "That was just the first step. Remember Grandpa Zeke also said that Mr. Dave's dad put those cool old vent covers over the new vents? Wouldn't that mean there would have been an open vent around here for a time?"

"I remember him doing that!" Mr. Dave exclaimed. "And I'm pretty sure it took a few days. There was a vent right there by that corner of the display case. Let me go get my hammer." Mr. Dave leaned his mop against the wall and left the lobby.

A big smile crossed Sam's face. "Otter! Do you think the Octopus has it?"

Otter grinned and shrugged. "Or maybe his replacement?"

Atim punched the air. "I can almost smell that pin! We're getting close!"

When Mr. Dave came back, he had a rubber mallet in his hand. He went to the wall by the display case. "My dad was a good carpenter. He lined up the wood, so you'd never know it was different. And then even the thin line where the join was would have been covered over by paint."

He tapped the wood in a few spots and cracks outlining a square appeared. With a few more whacks, the wood panel fell out and a dark hole appeared. The top end of a tin pipe could be seen.

Otter waved a hand at the hole. "That looks like the top of an Octopus arm!"

Mr. Dave reached in, but it came out empty. "Too far down. Let's all go downstairs."

Atim and Chickadee jumped with excitement. "We're going to see the Octopus!"

Sam slapped his face. "It's just a furnace!"

Otter laughed. "A furnace that may have eaten the pilfered pin!"

Mr. Dave led them downstairs. They were too excited to worry about monsters or spiders that might attack their ankles as they ran down the steps.

As Mr. Dave led them farther into the basement of the Factory Hall, he clicked on the ceiling lights. Finally, the Octopus stood, revealed in all its glory.

Chickadee looked slightly disappointed. "It *is* just an old furnace!"

Atim's eyes were huge. "Man!! It's a giant metal octopus, for sure! Look at those big nuts and bolts! They look like suckers. And the pipes, so cool—metal spaghetti arms!" He flung his arms around in the air.

Sam was studying the ceiling. "Which way is the front door, Otter?"

Otter lip-pointed past the Octopus. "It should be just a little farther that way."

Mr. Dave led them closer to the front wall of the basement. He began to tap on the pipes above his head. *Thunk, thunk. Thunk, thunk.*

They all followed the pipe along. Eventually, they came close to the elbow in the pipe that turned it upward to the vent.

Mr. Dave continued to tap the pipe. *Thunk, thunk. Thunk-tick, thunk-tick.*

He looked at the Muskrats. "Hear that?" He hit the pipe again. *Thunk-tick, thunk-tick.*

Sam had a big grin. "It sounds like something bounced after you hit the bottom of the pipe!"

Mr. Dave nodded. "Let me get some tools," he said. "I'm going to see if I can remove this length of pipe."

Chickadee clapped her hands. "It's like Christmas!"

Atim chuckled. "That's a heck of a party popper!"

Mr. Dave came back with screwdrivers, a chisel, and a crowbar. After fifteen minutes of grunting and groaning as he tried to loosen the pipe, he threw down the tools and left the room. In a moment, he returned with a sledge-hammer and some goggles.

Mr. Dave motioned for the Muskrats to move back. "You better go over there. I'm going to give it a good whack, and if it comes apart, who knows what's in there?"

Chickadee covered her nose. "A lot of dust, for sure."

When the cousins were far enough away, Mr. Dave hefted the sledgehammer and swung it at the pipe. *Clunk!*

After a few more tries, the end of the pipe came loose, and a cloud of dust enveloped Mr. Dave.

The detectives took a few more steps away from the cloud.

The old janitor reappeared. He coughed and waved the dust away from his face. "That may have worked a little too good."

He put down the big hammer and picked up the crowbar. Sunlight from the open vent on the first floor shone at the end of the pipe. With the crowbar in hand, Mr. Dave reached into the pipe and used the curved end to drag out anything that sat on its bottom.

Ka-ping-a-ling-a-ling!!

The not-pilfered pin hit the floor.

Chickadee cheered, Sam yelled, Atim howled, and Otter giggled.

A grinning Mr. Dave reached down, picked up the pin, and presented it to the Muskrats. "It was all of you that put this together. You figured out where it was. Everyone thought it was stolen. And here it was, in the arms of the Octopus the whole time."

EPILOGUE
Pin-pointed

A few weeks later, the Windy Lake Council Chambers were packed with people, including the Muskrats and their family.

The Chief looked around at those gathered. "With the head of the pin and the location of the hole it was in, we can now put to rest any assertion that the cottage area was not reserve land."

Everyone clapped and cheered.

When the din died down, the Chief turned to the Muskrats, who were dressed in their very best clothes.

"These little ones, these Mighty Muskrats, have done it again. We have something for them." She waved to her assistant, who brought out four beaded medallions. The Chief took them, and then held one up to the crowd for everyone to see.

The round medallion was a beaded replica of the top of the surveyor's pin. The date it was hammered into Picnic Creek Point and the boundaries of the Windy Lake reserve were included in the beading.

With cheers from the crowd, she placed one of the beaded necklaces over each head of the young detectives.

Atim held his up to everyone. "This is awesome!"

Chickadee held her medallion and rubbed her fingers over the smooth, glass beads. "It's beautiful and special all at the same time. A piece of history."

"Looks like we solved the case of the not-pilfered pin *and* the sad, old lady," Samuel said under his breath.

"It feels good to know we helped our people," Otter responded.

After the congratulations died down and a few more politicians spoke, everyone had some refreshments and then headed home.

The Muskrats tumbled into Grandpa's truck. As they rode, Chickadee couldn't help but ask, "Grandpa, are you happy to be reconnected to Ms. Lacroix?"

Grandpa smiled shyly. "Well, little one, it really was good to talk to an old friend. Life gets in the way sometimes, and our own fears and resentments too, of course. She invited me to the store for tea. I think I'll go."

The Muskrats giggled, happy that Grandpa had a "new" old friend.

They sat in silence for a little while. As they turned off the highway, a large rented moving van was visible at the corner. Its headlights flashed.

Looking around to make sure it was safe, Grandpa stopped alongside the van and rolled down his window.

Hayter Scott stuck his head out the moving van window. "Good to see you, old man." He waved his thumb over his shoulder. "All packed and heading out."

Grandpa frowned. "Where are you going?"

Mr. Scott shrugged a shoulder, and quickly glanced back the way he'd come. "I think it's time to leave. I was holding on to my father's dream. It wasn't really my own, I don't think. I'm not going to be…held a prisoner here, trying to live the life he wanted for himself."

Grandpa nodded his understanding. "We all change over the years."

Mr. Scott looked at the road beneath them. "Well, I hope I'm changing for the better now. And when I come back, it will be to visit you, my friend, on your lands."

Grandpa smiled and sighed. "That's good to hear, Hayter."

Mr. Scott stuck his head out a little farther and raised his voice. "I hear you kids found that surveyor's pin. That's amazing after all these years!"

Atim yelled back, "It was in the Octopus!!"

Mr. Scott laughed. "Of course it was. Well, I'm off. Take care, old man."

As the two vehicles moved away from each other, Grandpa looked at the children he loved so much. With his long, silver hair spilling around his shoulder, he smirked. "Let's hope you can teach old dogs new tricks."